FIRE PRINCESS

Hill City Heroes Book One

RACHEL BLAKE

Published by Blushing Books
An Imprint of
ABCD Graphics and Design, Inc.
A Virginia Corporation
977 Seminole Trail #233
Charlottesville, VA 22901

Rachel Blake
Fire Princess

EBook ISBN: 978-1-64563-062-3
Print ISBN: 978-1-64563-184-2
v2

Chapter 1

"New guy starts today! Do you think he's hot?"

Autumn rolled her eyes at her partner as she laced up her boots. "I think hot guys are the only kind who get hired at this station; unfortunately, most of them are married, may as well be married, or jerks."

"Did you hear that, guys?" one of the men in question shouted from the other side of the lockers. "Autumn thinks we are hot!"

"Damn right! Why else do you think I put up with this job? Sure as hell isn't the pay!" She slammed her locker shut and headed to the vacant great room. As she grabbed her favorite mug from its hiding place in the back of the cupboard, she headed for the coffee as she mumbled, "I need more coffee before they demand any more ego stroking."

"I call dibs."

The hunt for coffee halted. Empty mug in hand, she turned to face the other woman. "Did you seriously just call dibs on a man you have never met and know nothing about? Are we thirteen-year-old girls at a slumber party now?"

Gwen shoved Autumn away from the front of the

coffeemaker with a bump of her hip. "You're just mad you didn't call dibs first."

Laughter sounded from the other side of the room. "Do I get a say in this?" A man with dark hair walked toward them, his confidence and slight cockiness becoming clearer with every stride he took. "I'm the new guy, but you can call me Leland."

"Don't believe him; he's far from new and an old friend of mine," the chief, a forty-year-old man with a toned body that could grace the pages of any fireman calendar, said as he joined the growing group. He removed the coffeepot from the machine and filled both his and Autumn's cups. "He left our station a few years ago to work in a firehouse in Kansas City."

"And now you're back here? Are you crazy?" Autumn questioned as she wrapped her hands around the warming mug and took a sip.

"The city wasn't all it was cracked up to be, princess."

She glanced down at the mug in her hands and rolled her eyes at the plethora of miniature pink crowns and the word *Princess* stamped across it. "Well, congratulations, you can read, but don't call me that ever again if you want to keep your balls intact."

"As you wish, your highness."

His dramatic bow all but forced Autumn's eyes to roll into the back of her head before she tried to explain. "My best friend got this for me. I would have never bought it for myself."

"Good to know. Now, about this whole 'dibs' thing you girls were talking about?"

"That was her." Autumn pointed at her partner as she leaned against the counter next to the chief, casually sipping her coffee as she waited for the show to start.

A blush spread across the other woman's face. "I... you... I hate you, Autumn!"

"Oh, you *so* love me."

The corner of Leland's mouth curled into an evil smile as he

2

bracketed the blushing woman in place by resting his hands on the counter on either side of her hips. "Well, I have a couple of conditions if you are going to call dibs. First, you have to be a good cook."

"Oh, he can't cook, definitely gets docked points for that." Autumn's stage whisper forced a chuckle from the chief.

Leland glanced over his shoulder, daring her to continue. "I can cook; I just don't like to do it all the time. It's a duty I like to share." He turned back to the poor girl in front of him. "So can you cook?"

Straightening her spine, the woman gathered more bravado than Autumn knew her to have before she said, "I am an exceptionally good cook, but my baking will have you on your knees begging for more."

The chief coughed, choking on his coffee as Leland laughed outright at her boldness. "Oh, I never beg, but I have no objection to you doing so."

Her eyes narrowed a second before she stomped her foot. "Son of a bitch! You're one of them!"

"One of them?"

"A Dom!" She ducked under Leland's arm and turned to the chief. "For once, could you hire a vanilla man? Please? A simple, non-kinky, vanilla man." She started to stomp away but only got a few steps before she turned back with a shit-eating grin on her face. "You should talk to Autumn, though. She has been secretly going to clubs in the city for months now. You two may actually hit it off."

Coffee spewed from Autumn's mouth. "I. How. How do you know?"

"I have my ways." With those final words, she flounced away with her head held high.

Chapter 2

Autumn dug her phone out of her back pocket and wedged it between her ear and shoulder as she continued to limp toward the diner. "I know. I know. I'm late, and I promised I would be on time. I'm sorry!"

"I am going to kill you!" Sierra whispered from the other end before she spoke with a super sweet voice, no doubt an attempt to appease the disapproving look her brother was surely giving her from across the table. "I completely understand your job is important. You couldn't help that you got a call right before your shift ended."

"Come on; I apologized. I really couldn't help it."

"I know. How far away are you?"

Autumn looked at the street full of people and then at the diner door only a few shops away. "I'm a few blocks away. I will be there in five minutes."

"Okay. Hurry!"

Autumn shoved the phone back into her pocket then took a seat on a bench, alleviating some of the pain shooting up her leg; if it happened to prolong her friend's suffering just a bit, she was good with that, too. She had texted Sierra explaining why she

4

would be late, but it didn't sound like it placated her friend at all. All right, she was notoriously late to everything, but this time, it really wasn't her fault. As a paramedic, if she got a call while on shift, she had no choice but to go. Even if the call came in only fourteen minutes before the end of her 24-hour shift. It wasn't her fault the call took twice as long as usual. Okay, maybe she was to blame for the extra time, but it was not her fault she had become the second patient when she stepped in a hole and twisted her ankle. It also wasn't her fault that the chief had forced her to go to the ER and get her ankle checked out, forcing her to change her plans for their usual Sunday breakfast into a Sunday lunch.

"How long have you been sitting here?" Sierra questioned impatiently as she came to a stop in front of Autumn, her hands resting on her hips.

"Just since our call. Your brother that hard to deal with?" She gathered the other woman in a hard hug as she stood.

"He has been threatening to spank me since he sat down!"

Autumn laughed. "I still can't believe you let your brother spank you."

Sierra pushed Autumn back and held her at arm's length. "There is no 'letting.' This is just the way my family is. You do wrong, you get your butt blistered. End of story."

"Your brother, too?"

"Yeah, right! Who's going to spank that big brute? Now, come on, I want you to meet him. You are going to love him." Autumn followed the excited woman to the diner and to a table on the far side of the room. She stopped in her tracks when the man in the booth stood to greet her.

"Well, if it isn't the princess." Leland clumsily bowed in an exaggerated gesture before motioning for her to take her seat before seating himself. "You're my sister's best friend?"

Looking up from the scarred wood of the table, Autumn narrowed her eyes at the man. "Don't call me that!"

"You prefer that I call you your highness?"

She turned the question on him. "You're her big brother?"

"Wait." Leland turned to his sister as a smirk took over his handsome face. "That means *you* bought her the coffee mug."

"Yeah, isn't it awesome? 'I'm pretty sure I am supposed to be a princess; someone better fix this shit!' I laughed so hard when I saw it, and I had to get it for her. In fact, I got her two. One for home, one for the station." Sierra suddenly stopped talking and eyed the two of them. "Wait, how do you know about her mug?"

"He saw it."

The gears in Sierra's head were visibly turning. "How did he see it? You were working at the station last night."

Autumn smiled at the man, knowing the answer to her question already. "She doesn't know?"

"No. I didn't tell her. I needed a few days to get stuff situated without my baby sister and mother wanting to know every detail."

"Wait, wait, wait! You're confusing me. You saw her mug? At the fire station? What don't you want me to know?" When the pieces had finally all clicked together, Autumn watched as realization hit and hope lit her friend's face. "You are working at the station here in town! In Hill City? Why didn't you tell me!"

"Because you would overreact."

"Hold on! Does this mean you're moving home?"

"No, it means I am moving back to the 'home' area. I close on my house in three weeks."

Sierra's squeal of excitement forced a few people in the dinner to cover their ears. "My brother's moving back! He's back! He's coming home!" She stood and did her happy dance in the narrow space between the tables. After a few seconds, Leland reached out and popped her once on the ass. "Ow!"

"It is evident that my being home is way overdue. Behave like the young lady you are, or I will give you another." With a pout, Sierra plopped down in the booth next to the shocked Autumn.

"Wipe that scowl off your face and properly introduce me to the princess over here."

"I thought you already met?"

"No, I just saw her once yesterday morning, and I barely got her name. I never saw her again after the first meeting unless you count getting a glimpse of her ass as she ran out of the room. I think she was avoiding me on purpose," Leland teased, looking at Autumn out of the corner of his eye.

Before Autumn could think better of it, she had kicked the man under the table. "I was not avoiding you. What reason would I have to do that?" She tilted her head toward her friend, and she prayed he would get the message she was trying so desperately to convey.

Sierra sighed as she picked up her menu and spoke from behind it like the conversation bored her. "No need to physically assault him, Autumn. I'm smarter than you give me credit for. I know all about my brother's sexual preferences. Eww." A shiver ran through her body. "Didn't want to have this conversation today. Anyway, I also know you have been visiting the same kind of clubs he secretly frequents when in town." She set her menu down, and a satisfied expression graced her face as she looked between the two of them. "While the two of you may be strangers to each other, I know you both *very* well, and you both suck at hiding stuff from me."

Autumn turned to Sierra, once again, stunned. "You know about me going to the clubs?"

"Of course, I do."

"How?"

"I have my sources, and I am not about to give them up."

Leland shook his head as he picked up his own menu. "Why does everyone keep bringing up our sexual preferences, princess?"

"You call me that one more time, and I am going to kick you

so hard that you will not need to worry about your sexual preferences for a while."

He just tossed his head back and laughed.

"OKAY, spill. You have to tell me how you know about me going to the OYK," Autumn demanded as she trailed Sierra out of the restaurant.

"I'm keeping that information to myself. My source, or sources, trust me to keep his, her, or their identities a secret. If I don't, they could lose their standing in the community."

"At least tell me what else they told you!"

"Not a chance. I have to have a few tricks up my sleeve," Sierra said before nervously fingering her necklace. "So what happened at the station?"

"Nothing."

"I call bullshit! You complain about everyone being stacked on top of each other at the firehouse all the time. Yet my brother only saw you once during your whole 24-hour shift together? Like I said, bullshit! So, you may as well tell me before I come to my own conclusion, which would be much worse than the truth."

Autumn turned her face to the sun and let the light warm her skin. Heaving a heavy sigh with her eyes still closed against the brightness, she spoke. "I wasn't ready for anyone to know about my trips to the clubs. I wanted to have a chance to find myself in the giant world of kink before I had to explain my choices to anyone."

"I am the last person you would have to explain yourself to."

Hearing the thread of hurt that ran through Sierra's words, Autumn peeked at her friend then gathered the woman in her arms. "It wasn't you who I didn't want to explain my sex life to. People at work, my parents, people I don't necessarily trust my feelings with—they are who I didn't want to tell."

"What? I know them, so I'm guilty by association?"

Autumn ignored her whining. "You know me. You know if I am going to do something, I have to do it all the way. When I find the right Dominant man, I'm not going to be his submissive just behind closed doors. I will be his all the time. It will lead to looks and whispers, and I was not ready for that yet, so I kept it to myself." She paused for a second before continuing with a whine of her own. "A lot of good that did me. Somehow, my partner at the station found out. In fact, when your brother said he was a Dom, she outed my submissiveness right there in front of him *and* the chief."

"You're shitting me!" Sierra shoved Autumn back, shock clear on her face.

"Not at all."

"What happened?"

"It was *so* awkward! I avoided them all day," Autumn mumbled from behind her hands, her face flaming.

Sierra tried to hide her laugh for all of two seconds before it erupted from her chest. "I'm sorry. I shouldn't laugh, but it is perfect."

"No! Perfect does not belong anywhere near that sentence."

"You will know what I mean soon enough." She hesitated for a second before changing the subject. "I know this is selfish of me, but are you still willing to distract him tonight while I go on my date? If you don't want to hang out with him after the scene at the firehouse, I completely understand. I will just go behind his back and tell my mom he's in town. She will keep him busy."

"As entertaining as that sounds, don't. I will hang out with him. How much more embarrassed can I be? Just promise me my ass will be safe."

"Promise. As for mine, on the other hand, I cannot say the same."

"You could just tell him you are too old for spankings, especially the non-sexy kind from your brother."

"Yes, because that went over so well the last time," Sierra retorted, releasing a long sigh. "No, as much as I hate to admit it, I need him and the weird dynamic we have. At least until I find a man willing to take over."

"I am very glad to hear you say that," Leland rumbled from behind the duo, making them both squeal in surprise.

"Geez! Do you make it a habit to sneak up on people like that?" Autumn scolded as she clutched at her chest.

"It is the only way I find out what is going on in my favorite and littlest sister's life," he teased as he slung his arm around the little sister in question.

Sierra rolled her eyes. "I am the only sister you have, and before you start the lecture about putting family first, you called me twelve hours ago from what I thought was your car, but apparently, you were at your new job. There is no way you could actually believe that is enough time for me to change my plans for tonight."

"I'm your big brother! You should drop everything and keep me company for the night."

"You're my only brother, and if you were just here for a couple of days, I would do just that, but didn't you hear, you're moving home?"

Leland reared back and covered his ears when she screamed the last part. "Sounds like I arrived here just in the nick of time. It seems to me that Dad has let you get away with far too much."

Sierra ignored his comment. "Now, don't worry about finding something to do while I am on my date because Autumn has agreed to keep you company while I'm gone."

Leland peered from his sister to Autumn and then back again as if contemplating whether it was a reasonable trade-off. "Okay. Who knows? Maybe we will find her missing tiara."

Chapter 3

Autumn studied the clock again for the hundredth time that night. *The stupid thing must have stopped working.* It said she still had fifteen minutes until he was due to arrive, but there she stood in her favorite pair of jeans, the ones that made her butt look its best, and a fitted tee shirt, waiting for him at the door like a puppy who had been left at home all day.

When she had told him that she would like to avoid the gossip that going to a restaurant in town would create, he thankfully agreed to hang out at his sister's house and order a pizza. When she told him she would be there at seven, his attitude became anything but agreeable.

"My mama would have a fit if she knew I allowed you to drive yourself," he said as his sister shook her head slowly as if she knew exactly how this conversation would go.

"Allowed? I am perfectly capable of driving myself a few blocks. Hell, I will probably just walk it." The groan from Sierra let Autumn know she had said the completely wrong thing.

"You will not drive, and you absolutely will *not* walk in the dark. You will allow me to pick you up like the proper gentleman my mother painstakingly taught me to be."

"But it really isn't—" Autumn got cut short by the growl that vibrated from deep within Leland's chest. With a huff, she agreed. "Fine! Bossy Doms, anyway." The last mumbled part of her reply got her an eyebrow lift from Leland and a snort of laughter from Sierra.

At the sound of the doorbell, Autumn jumped. She quickly checked her purse for her debit card one last time before reaching for the door, but that was all the farther she got. When her hand touched the knob, she froze as her sneaky best friend's plan hit her right in the forehead. Sierra had set her up. The brat was trying to set Autumn up with her brother.

"Unless you plan on talking to me through the door all night, you may have to open it. Turn the knob, princess," Leland teased from the other side of the door.

Wrenching the door open, she shot the man a dirty look. "You know, it is unkind to mock people. Especially the individual who volunteered to keep you company for the evening despite your tendency to be an ass."

"Watch the language, princess. I do not take kindly to being sworn at, and those words falling from your mouth are anything but attractive." Autumn felt the blush spread across her face as Leland offered her his arm as if he had not just scolded her for her potty-mouth. "Now, my dear, I believe we have a date with a pepperoni and mushroom pizza and a movie of your choosing."

AUTUMN COULDN'T CONTAIN her full belly laugh when a blood-curdling scream echoed through the house. "Holy shit!" Leland roared as a particularly gory scene came to an end and the credits started rolling. She continued to laugh as Leland glared at her accusingly. "I thought you said you had never seen this movie before!"

"I never said that. I have seen it so many times that your sister refuses to watch it with me anymore. She says I suck all the fun out of it when I don't jump at the scary parts."

"Or it could be because she is a scaredy-cat and despises scary movies."

"No, she loves them. She watches them with me all the time."

"And then I'm on the phone with her all night telling her that vampires or ax murderers or sadistic cults are not going to invade her bedroom in the night." Leland laughed as he stood from his chair. "How about a stroll?"

"I thought I wasn't allowed to walk outside at night," Autumn sassed from the couch.

"You are prohibited from walking at night without me. Now, get your shoes on, brat."

As soon as they stepped out into the dark, the cool night air wrapped itself around them, and the smell of fall tickled her nostrils. Leland turned his face to the sky, and Autumn could do nothing to stop the slightly teasing tone in her voice. "Lee, you aren't going to see any stars from here; the lights are too bright."

He smiled at her, looping his arm around her waist and propelling her forward. "I like the way that nickname sounds when you say it."

"Your sister will be disappointed." Autumn laughed as she wiggled away from his grasp before allowing herself to become accustomed to it. "She had hoped that my calling you Lee would annoy you like it does when she says it."

"No, because you didn't repeat it like a broken record for six months. I kid you not! She was seven and the only thing she said for *months* was Lee. My parents thought something was wrong with her until the day they took her to the doctor and she called him a fucking nut job before running out of the office. That is why I don't like it when my brat of a sister calls me Lee." He allowed Autumn her laugh at his expense, then he changed the subject. "I can't wait to step out onto the deck at night and be able to see the stars twinkling in the sky. Hell, that's part of the reason I bought the house I did."

"Your house is in the country?" At his nod, she continued. "Where? I have been searching for a house outside city limits for months and haven't found anything other than run-down, old farmhouses where even the field mice aren't interested in living."

"I found out a few months ago that the station I worked out of in Kansas City was closing. They offered me a transfer to another station in the city, but before I accepted the new position, the chief informed me of the opening here. I couldn't pass up the opportunity to be closer to my family, so I applied and got the job last month. I bought a house and some property from a friend of mine, and here I am."

"Sierra is really excited you are going to be close. For reasons I have yet to figure out, she misses you when you're gone."

"I would like to know how, in all the times I have been home for a visit, I have not met you before now? She talks about you all the time, so I would have thought we would have met."

"She doesn't like to share." Autumn snickered.

"Oh, I know."

"Now, back to this house. If you tell me you have no neighbors, you may end up with a roommate."

Leland chuckled. "The couple I bought the property from lives across the street, and they are the only neighbors I have. Other than that, the closest neighbor is a mile away. I've known them forever. They are good people, so I think I can handle having them so close."

"I envy you."

"Well, if you ever need to get out of town and away from the noisy neighbors, you are more than welcome to come out."

Just as Autumn opened her mouth to reply, she stepped on a rock and rolled the same ankle she had hurt that morning.

"Are you all right?"

"Yeah," Autumn replied smoothly as a sharp pain shot up her calf. "I want to thank you for the invitation, but I must also warn you, you may end up regretting the offer."

"I doubt there will ever be a point in my life where I regret inviting you to my house."

"If I didn't know any better, Leland Boisy, I would think you were hitting on me."

"That's because I *am* hitting on you." Her steps faltered. "Easy, pet. We don't need any accidents."

"I. Did. Did you just admit you were hitting on me?"

"I did," he readily confessed as he easily stared into her eyes.

Autumn gaped at the man. "How can you do that so easily?"

"Do what?"

"Be so open and honest without any thought of what may happen if I don't react well to it?"

"I am a firm believer in communication. In the lifestyle, openness and honesty are vital, or someone could get hurt."

"What exactly is your lifestyle? I mean, I know you're a Dom, but when you picture your relationship, what do you see?" Autumn felt the hope curl in her belly.

"I am a Dominant, but what I want in a relationship is still unknown to me. I do know that I want a woman who will respect and obey me in more than just the bedroom, but I don't want a slave. I want to know that when we are with our friends who are also in the lifestyle, and I tell her to suck my cock, she will do it."

Autumn tripped. Luckily, Leland was quick enough to catch her by the back of her pants just before she hit the sidewalk with her face. "Thanks."

The next word out of his mouth was little more than a growl, "Careful."

Why couldn't she convince herself to look the man in the eye? She could make eye contact just fine a few seconds ago.

"You're avoiding my eyes, princess. Is this going to become a habit? You avoiding me when we start talking about our sexual preferences?"

"Probably." Realizing what he had said, she looked up at him. "You plan on talking about our sexual preferences on a regular basis?"

"I do, pet." That was the second time he had called her by that name, and this time, she could do nothing to prevent the hitch in her breath as the pet name rolled off his tongue. "Don't act surprised. You know the whole reason my sister 'went out' tonight was so she would have an excuse to push us together."

"I take it she has set you up like this before?"

"Way too many times to count, but with you, it's different."

"How?" A bout of pain engulfed her ankle as she asked the question, causing her question to come out sounding a little strangled.

"You're her best friend. She isn't going to set you up for failure."

"She has set you up for failure multiple times, and you're her brother."

"This time is different. She has a vested interest in both of us. She didn't care about any of the other women she set me up with, but you. You are the sister she never had." Leland clutched his chest. "As much as it pains me to say this, she loves you as much as she does me." Autumn had to laugh at his dramatics. "Are you laughing at me, sub?"

"Only if you want me to, Sir." She barely got the words out before she bent at the waist and dissolved into another fit of laughter.

He scowled at her for about half a second until an enormous, breathtaking smile took over his handsome mug. "So how often do you go to the club?"

"*The* club? I go to *a* club once or twice a month. I have gone to many BDSM clubs."

Leland gripped her arm and turned her to face him, all

traces of his previous smile gone. "Tell me you that once you discovered OYK, that is the only club you've gone to since."

"That would be a lie," Autumn stated as she pulled herself from his grasp. She started to limp away, cursing her inability to walk normally and leaving Leland no choice but to follow.

"Promise me you will stay away from them. I don't frequent clubs often, but I know none of the others around here have the security and safety that OYK does."

"I don't know if I can do that, either," Autumn replied honestly. "I agree, the other places lack many safety measures when compared to OYK, but the membership fees are too expensive for me, and I refuse to stop exploring BDSM altogether. I made a promise to myself to explore this to my fullest extent, and that is a promise I intend to keep."

"While you are dating me, you will not go to *any* club without me, and the only one we will go to together is OYK."

"While we are dating?" She knew the expression on her face dared him to repeat his statement, but it quickly became apparent he was not going to do so. "I don't remember you ever asking me out."

"That *was* me asking."

Autumn eyed the cocky man. "We *really* need to start working on your technique, big boy. That was *the* worst way *anyone* has *ever* asked me out in my *entire* life. It even beats out the time in fifth grade when I got a note passed to me asking me to circle yes or no."

Leland chuckled for the briefest second before he stopped and grasped Autumn's hand in his own. "Let's see where this one ranks."

Her retort was unable to slip past her lips because before she knew what was happening, Leland had captured her mouth in a searing kiss that quickly turned rough. He nipped at her lips. She boldly bit back, but when she tried to pull away, he had none of it and clasped the back of her head. His firm hold quickly turned her into a compliant captive, giving him exactly what he wanted. He grazed his teeth along her lip again, much gentler this time, and she allowed herself to become lost in the kiss. When her knees buckled, he wrapped his arms around her and placed his hands on the curves of her ass, lifting her to her toes and pressing her body against his.

Autumn would have sworn she heard a growled, "Mine," rumble from deep within Leland's chest, but before she could question it, pain had flared in her ankle as a result of the changed position, and she winced.

She knew she didn't imagine the unhappy grumble that rattled within his chest as he placed her on her feet once more. She did her best to hide the flinch, but he saw it. He stepped back and eyed her up and down with worry etched on his face. "Did I hurt you?" Autumn's stomach dropped to her toes as her eyes fell to his chest. "Eyes here."

Autumn inhaled unsteadily and raised her eyes to meet his. "No, you did nothing to hurt me. I twisted my ankle on the call I ran this morning."

"Why didn't you tell me you were having trouble with your ankle before we left the house? We didn't have to take a walk."

"My ankle felt fine."

His eyes narrowed the slightest bit. "Then why are you wincing every time I move you? Wait, you got hurt on a call? Tell me you reported it to Chief."

Autumn sighed. "He knows. In fact, he escorted me to the ER."

"Probably to be sure you did as you were told." Autumn rolled her eyes. "First rule, my sub does not roll her eyes at me unless she wants to feel my displeasure at her blatant disrespect upon her ass."

Her eyes skirted away from his eyes once more. "I haven't agreed yet."

"I know. Now, give me your eyes again, thank you, and then tell me what the doctor told you."

"The doctor said I would be fine." When he quirked his brow, she continued. "But I should rest it for the next day or so."

"What is your middle name?"

The jump in subject confused her a bit. "Rose. Why?"

"Autumn Rose Johnson, you need to do as the doctor tells you!"

Autumn groaned and rolled her eyes again. The chief had given her another version of the same lecture only hours before.

"Oh, little subbie, you are so lucky you have yet to agree to be mine." As soon as he finished talking, he bent at the waist and put his shoulder into her stomach. Lifting her into the air, he turned back in the direction they came.

A squeal of surprise escaped from between Autumn's lips as her world went topsy-turvy when he unceremoniously tossed her over his shoulder. Her fists bounced off his back as she yelled at him, "Put me down! Put me down, right now, you jackass. I am perfectly capable of walking." In response to her demand and word choice, a hand bounced off her ass, leaving behind only the slightest sting, but the surprise silenced her.

"You may think you are capable of walking, but you are obviously incapable of doing as you are directed. Tell me, do you disobey everyone or just your doctor?"

"I don't have anyone to answer to, so I have no need to do as I'm told."

His voice softened drastically. "I am hoping that will change after tonight, princess."

The rest of the walk was silent except for Autumn's occasional grunts when his steps forced a bit of air from her lungs. The rhythmic motion of his gait was surprisingly relaxing and allowed her mind to wander. He had asked her out. He may have gone about it in the wrong way, but he had done so nonetheless.

He had asked her, even knowing she was relatively new to the lifestyle.

Did she want to date him? With nearly every fiber of her being, she did, but the tiny voice in the back of her head told her that she needed to know more. She needed to know what his expectations for this relationship were.

Hell, did he want a relationship or just a play partner? If he desired the latter, she would have to turn him down. There was no way she would be able to be physically involved with this man and, at the same time, keep her emotions in check. She wouldn't do that to herself.

"Are you sleeping up there?" Leland teased as he wedged his hand into the pocket of her jeans, pulling her from her thoughts as he pulled the key from her pocket.

"I could have gotten it. There was no reason to grope me," Autumn complained as she pushed her unruly dark hair out of her face so she could scowl at the man unhindered.

The sound of Leland's laughter had her belly fluttering. "I asked for the key twice before I took matters into my own hands."

When he swung the door open, Autumn expected him to put her down, but instead, he kicked the door shut behind him and headed to the living room. "Your sister is going to kick your ass when she finds out you wore shoes on her rug."

"That is why I am going to keep that information to myself, and so are you."

"Oh, I'm totally telling," Autumn countered as he set her on the sofa with a smirk.

He knelt in front of her, gently placing her foot on his thigh before he started working the laces of her Converse sneakers loose. "I am sure you will, princess. Now, let's see how much damage you have done. With how gently I removed your shoe, there should have been no reason for you to wince like you did. Not what I like to see." He palpitated the slightly swollen joint before he snatched a pillow from beside her. Placing it on the coffee table, he gently set her foot on top. "I am not happy you kept this from me. Stay there."

With that, he strode away. Autumn strained to hear what he was doing, but the pounding of her heart drowned out all other sounds as her heart rate climbed. Did he leave? Was their non-date over?

He had just left her there with an order to stay put. Yes, she could get up and leave, or see what he was doing, but he told her to stay there. As stupid as it sounded to her, she didn't want to disappoint him. Her need for his approval meant he might as well have tied her down. Would Sierra return later to find her still sitting on the couch waiting for Leland?

"I finally found something that will pass as ice," Leland said as he walked back in the room, causing Autumn to jump. When his eyes met hers, he nearly ran to her. "Autumn, what's wrong?"

The concern in his voice touched her heart. "Nothing's wrong. I-I just didn't know where you went."

He knelt in front of her once more and placed a towel-wrapped bag on top of her ankle. "I just went to the kitchen to find some ice or something to put on your ankle. I didn't think it would take ten minutes." He rolled his eyes. "There is nothing of nutritional value in her kitchen. The mixed vegetables that are on your ankle right now were spilled all over the back of her freezer."

Autumn's mouth dropped open. "Why do you get to roll your eyes, and I can't?"

"You can roll your eyes, but if you decide to be mine, it would be a risky habit to continue. May be wise to start curbing it now, because you are going to say yes, eventually."

"What exactly does being yours mean?"

"It means we date like a vanilla couple does, but it also means we set out our expectations and rules for this relationship beforehand. You need to know what I expect of you, and I need to know what you want and expect from me."

"So is this when we negotiate?"

"Are you saying you are willing to give this a chance?"

"I am saying that you have my attention, and I am willing to hear you out."

"That is all I can ask. For now, anyway."

Chapter 4

As she was bent over and backing out of the freshly scrubbed ambulance, Autumn nearly jumped out of her skin when a hand came down hard on her ass. She spun on her attacker, sitting on the sopping wet floor of the rig in the process, and glared at the man. "I swear to all that is holy, Davis, if you touch my ass one more time, I will knock you on yours!"

"Relax, Johnson. I was just trying to tell you good job out there." The man in question held his arm in the air in a placating gesture.

"Don't try to act all innocent with me. I have been shooting down your advances for way too long. Keep your hands to yourself."

"Is there a problem here?" Leland questioned as he joined the two of them previously unseen from the side of the rig, causing both to startle.

"No, I was just telling Autumn what a good job she did at the scene. The woman has a fighting chance because of her quick thinking."

Autumn rolled her eyes but resisted the urge to bang her

head against one of the cabinets in the ambulance. "Laying it on a bit thick, are you?"

"No," Leland interjected before he turned his displeased look on Autumn. "He is right about you saving the woman. When we pulled her out of that truck, we thought she was a goner, but after a few minutes with you, she had signs of life. You did good work, Autumn." His face hardened even further before he turned back to Davis. "But if I catch your hands on her or any of the other females at the station again, I will go after your job, and I will succeed."

Davis's lip curled in disdain as he spun on his heels and stormed away.

"Thank you, but I have been dealing with that infuriating man for years. You didn't need to get involved."

"Of course, I am going to get involved. I want you to be mine, so I am going to treat you like such until you tell me to hit the road. And I protect what's mine."

Autumn, of course, rolled her eyes. It had been two weeks since their non-date. They had worked six shifts together, and his insistent nagging was starting to wear her down. The man was devious in the way he did it, too. He started out as a gentleman, allowing her to enter a room before him or offering her his seat, but those small gestures soon grew, and before she knew it, he was treating her as one would a girlfriend.

On their non-date, they had agreed on all the rules and expectations they would have in their D/s relationship, but she had told him that she needed time to think. He agreed to give her that time, but he had slowly started incorporating some D/s related warnings into their everyday routine at the station. The first time he had spanked her was on their fourth shift together.

They were working a car accident that night, and she had forgotten to put on her reflective vest. Combine that with her pumping adrenaline and just plain stupidity, and she had nearly been hit by a passing vehicle on her way back to the rig. Leland had snagged her by the back of her jacket just in time. After assuring that she was unharmed, he landed three hard swats to her ass before he gave her a light push toward their visibly pissed off chief.

After that incident, and the resulting reprimand, Leland quit holding back. He made it known to all that Autumn was off-limits, and with most of the guys on their shift practicing the life-style in some way or another, nearly everyone heeded his notice. Davis was the exception.

"I *hate* when you roll those lovely hazel eyes at me," Leland growled as he pinched her hard on the ass.

"That is why I can't say yes to you," Autumn chastised as she threw the wad of used paper towels at his chest.

"Because I don't like it when you roll your eyes?"

"No, because you rebuke me at work. I have a job to do here, and I cannot have you smacking my ass every time you don't like a decision I make while at said job. I would become the laughing stock of the station."

"First off, I know you are an excellent paramedic, and I would never inhibit your work with my barbaric ways. And before you say it, I know I landed some smacks on your butt when you nearly killed yourself the other night, but in my defense, you scared the *shit* out of me. If I had not smacked your ass a few times, I know Kevin would have." The truth in his words rang true. Chief Atwood acted much like an older brother to her at times, and he would have no problem laying a couple of butt burners upon her seat. He had done it before, not that she would ever admit it to him. "Second, all but a few of these men here are part of my inner circle. I have been friends with them for years, which means I have and *will* play with my sub in front of them. I have played with some of their subs in the past, and not a single one of these men will use our lifestyle as a tool against you."

"What about Davis?"

"He is far from my inner circle and will never know what we do or believe in."

"So you won't discipline me at work?"

The corner of the man's mouth turned up. "I never said that. Will I embarrass you or spank you in front of people while we are at work? No. Will I reprimand you for a choice you make regarding a patient? Never. Not even at home. I will, however, paddle your ass red if you endanger your life like that again. I will take any sass, including eye rolling, into consideration and decide if it was just playful banter among colleagues or a subbie in need of correction. But know, if you show too much sass in front of the guys I—we—trust, I won't hesitate to land a swat on your butt."

Autumn's mouth dropped open. "You just said you would never spank me in front of people while we are at work."

"Oh, Autumn, that swat would not be a spanking. It would be a warning."

Autumn stood there, weighing her options. She could tell him she was uninterested, and he would respect that, but if just the thought of refusing him had her stomach roiling, there was no way she would be able to get the words out. "Yes."

"Yes." Leland drew out the word, apparently wanting her to elaborate.

"Yes, I would like to try both dating you in the vanilla world and as a D/s couple."

She had just finished talking when his hands landed on her hips and she became airborne. She clutched his shoulders in an attempt to balance herself as Leland held her above his head as if she weighed nothing and spun in a circle before he placed her back on her feet and landed a hard kiss on her lips.

Of course, the chief decided to wander into the truck bay and cleared his throat at that precise moment. Autumn took a hurried step back, tripped over some unrolled hose and landed hard on her ass on the concrete floor. She would have covered her blushing face with her hands if she was not still wearing soiled gloves.

"Shit, Johnson, are you okay?" Chief asked as his steps ate up the distance between them and he offered her his hand. It was an unnecessary gesture as Leland was already physically picking her up off the floor.

"Would you quit picking me up?" Autumn chided as she roughly shoved his hands away from where they still rested on her hips. "I am far too heavy for you to pick up like that." A swat to her canvas covered bottom followed her words. "Hey!"

"Warning. You put yourself down like that again, and I will get inventive with my implement of choice. Got it?"

"Yes, Sir," Autumn replied as she glanced at the toe of her scuffed, black boot, utterly embarrassed that he had a reason to reproach her in front of the chief, even if it was only a swat.

"Don't be embarrassed on my behalf, Autumn. I have had to get after my own wife more than a few times for the same thing, and I am sure that will not be the only time I see him show you how truly displeased he is with you," Chief Atwood reassured, somehow knowing exactly what she had been thinking.

"But that will be different. You won't be standing in front of me with your uniform, announcing that you are my boss the next time. Well, I hope not."

Kevin laughed. "No, but I will, more than likely, be completely immersed in my role as a Dom, and I will still be the boss. The only difference is that Lee will outrank *me* when it comes to you." With a gentle smile, Kevin meandered away, giving her arm a reassuring squeeze on his way past.

Leland wrapped his arms around Autumn, giving her no choice but to press her face into his chest as he rubbed her butt as if he were soothing away the sting from his strike. "It will never be okay for you to talk badly about yourself, princess."

"I can't decide if I hate you calling me that or love it."

"If you really hate it, I will stop using it."

"No!" Her response was quick and sharp as she lifted her head from his chest. "I said I may love it, too. You can keep calling me princess. I mean, after all, I need to hear it a few more times before I make up my mind."

"Good. I wasn't ready to give it up," Leland replied with laughter in his voice. Just as Autumn opened her mouth to give a retort, the tone sounded.

"We have a report of a vehicle versus vehicle accident on the corner of Train and Gibson Street. All units, please respond," a disembodied voice announced as the couple parted ways and the rest of the department poured into the bay.

Autumn climbed into the passenger side of the ambulance and watched Leland pull on his bunkers through the side mirror.

"You know," Gwen started as she climbed into the driver's seat. "It would be highly inappropriate for you to jump his bones in the middle of the call."

"Gwen! I would never do that!"

"Really? Because that look on your face tells me you totally would."

Chapter 5

"You have to tell her we are dating," Leland demanded as he ambled through the kitchen with a box in his arms.

"I will," Autumn whispered harshly as she shoved a stack of dishes into the cupboard above her head.

"It has been a week since you agreed to be mine, and I am sick of hiding it from my sister. You will do it. Now." The unspoken "or else" hung in the air long after Leland left the room.

With a sigh, she shut the cabinet and rested her head against the cool wood. Leland had offered to talk to his sister the day after they became a couple, but Autumn had begged him to let her do it. She had every intention of telling her best friend about their relationship, but the words had failed her every time she tried.

A smack to her left butt cheek instantly had Autumn straightening from her slightly bent over position. "Ow!"

Leland stood there with his arms crossed over his chest. "You leave it out there like that, then I have no choice but to assume you are in need of a little encouragement to do as you were told."

"You. I. You hit me!"

"I spanked you. Big difference. And I am going to do it again, repeatedly, if you don't get your ass out to that moving truck and tell my sister we are dating."

"I will tell her when we have all your things moved in."

"No, you will tell her now." Leland pulled Autumn away from the counter and gave her ass another swat to get her moving in the right direction.

When Autumn turned to give him the "what for" look, two things stopped her. The solemn expression on his face and the man who stood behind him failing miserably in his attempt to hide his smirk. With a sulk firmly in place, Autumn went to do his bidding.

"Sierra, can I talk to you for a moment?" Autumn called when she got close enough to be heard.

"Sure, what's up?" Sierra questioned as she spun around, clipboard in hand.

"Who knew Leland could get so many guys rounded up to help him move?"

"I know. Between the guys from the station and their girlfriends and wives, we are going to be finished in no time. Oh, those go to the kitchen," Sierra said, directing the tall man with two boxes. "Thank God Dad demanded that their trip to Florida not be changed. My mother would be in a constant state of blushing with all the swearing."

"Speaking of girlfriends, I—"

"Autumn, I'm an intelligent woman. I know you're dating my brother." Sierra laughed at her friend. "Unless you plan on catching flies, I suggest you close your mouth."

"How did you know?"

"You guys suck at sneaking around," Sierra explained as she pointed another man in the right direction.

"We didn't 'suck' at hiding our relationship. Hell, I only agreed to date him a week ago."

The "are you kidding me" look she shot Autumn's way made her feel a little naïve. "The man has been living with me for three weeks. If you were not at my house, my brother would mysteriously disappear only to return late at night, if at all. Don't get me started on the way you two acted when you were at the house. You may as well have been in his lap half the time. Do you know how many times I saw him give you *the* look when you got a little too lippy for his liking?"

"He never gave me *the* look!"

"That same look has been directed at me too many times, so trust me when I say he gave you *the* look. Didn't take a genius to figure it out that you were shacking up with my brother. And do you really believe it has only been a week? It has only been a week since you *agreed*, but he owned you long before that, and everyone *except* you knew it."

"First of all, there has been no 'shacking up.' Second, why didn't you say anything?" Autumn questioned, choosing to ignore the last statement.

"It was fun watching you guys sneak around like a couple of teenagers just to keep little old me out of the loop. Now that it is officially official, it is my best friend duty to let you know that my big brother doesn't put up with *any* nonsense. While you two are dating, your butt will never be safe from his itchy palm. He's not one of those wannabe Doms you have dated in the past who let you have your way as soon as you bat your eyelashes at them." Sierra shook her head. "Leland is the head of his house, a man of his word, and will be in charge of your relationship. He will take charge of more than just your bedroom activities."

"A little late with the warning about his hard hand," Autumn whined as she reached back to rub the still tender spot on her butt.

"I am *so* glad you are dating him. Maybe you will keep him

busy enough that he will forget about my need to be straightened out every once in a while." Sierra's teasing smile slipped away as she took a deep breath and studied her feet. "I also didn't tell you I knew because when I did, I would have to tell you about my own kink, and I wasn't ready for that yet."

"Your need to be spanked is old news to me," Autumn joked as she bumped Sierra's hip with her own.

"I am not just submissive, Autumn. I am a little."

A soft smile spread across Autumn's face as she gave her friend a hug and whispered in her ear, "You suck at hiding stuff from me, too." Autumn walked away, giggling at the stunned expression on her friend's face.

"YOU TWO CAN STAY for the party, but there are some rules."

Autumn rolled her eyes. She'd better be allowed to stay for the party. She had worked hard to get this man moved into his new house, and how did he repay her? He had her and his sister sitting side by side on the couch so he could lay out the rules. What were they, kids about to be let loose with the family car for the first time?

"Stand," Leland commanded as soon as Autumn's eyes focused back on him.

She bit her lip and shot a quick glance at Sierra, who showed absolutely no sympathy as Autumn did as she was told. She was used to being with a Dom at the clubs, but it was taking longer than she hoped to curb her sass in an everyday setting.

"Turn around." Leland twirled his finger in the air menacingly.

As soon as she was facing away from him, he stepped to her left side and landed ten hard, well-placed smacks to each thigh just under the hem of her shorts. She did her best to stay still, but the need to dance on her tiptoes got the best of her.

"Just as well. I was trying to decide how to let everyone know you were off-limits tonight. What better way than to have my handprints on the back of your legs?"

Autumn peered over her shoulder and tried to speak as politely as she could. "Sir? You couldn't have just told them that I was off-limits for the night?"

"He needed to stake his claim before he let you loose."

Autumn watched as Leland gave his sister a knowing smile before she spoke. "I thought you said everyone knew I belonged to him weeks ago?"

"Oh, they did, but his marks on your ass will be like a flashing neon sign showing all who care to know that he isn't sharing. For tonight, anyway."

Autumn's mouth dropped open as she looked back and forth between the siblings, trying to determine if she was joking. Finally, she asked, "You share?"

"I have in the past, yes, but I am not sure I am going to be so willing with you. The thought of someone else fucking you brings my blood to a boil," Leland reassured before he threw the next curve ball at her. "However, the thought of watching someone paddle that beautiful ass of yours makes me impossibly hard."

"Eww!" Sierra squealed as she covered her ears with her hands, closed her eyes and started to hum to herself as she rocked.

Leland rolled his eyes at his sister's antics before his face grew stern and he turned back to his wayward girlfriend, obviously ready to get back to the original topic. "If you are going to curb your attitude, you may sit back down. If not, you can bend over the arm of the couch and receive your first proper spanking from me."

"I will behave." As soon as he nodded his head, Autumn sat on the sofa. She wasn't about to give him the chance to change his mind.

"The only added rule I have for you two is that you are only allowed one drink."

"What?" Sierra exclaimed, shock and annoyance clearly expressed on her face.

"If you want to stay here, that is the condition, but you should know that Zander's flavor of the week is on her way out here." Sierra's eye narrowed slightly, but she nodded her agreement. Leland's attention returned to Autumn. "This isn't a play party, but everyone here is part of the lifestyle in some way or another. I don't want you to be shocked if a sub mouths off one too many times and you witness a punishment." Autumn nodded her head as a slight blush spread across her face. "Don't forget our rules, princess, and you will be just fine."

"Yes, Sir."

Leland turned to his sister as a smile split his face. "If you think you can deal with Zander and his latest fling, then Tabitha wants you to join her on the deck."

"She's here?" All it required was a single nod of Leland's head, and Sierra was off the couch and headed for the back door. "Tabby!"

"Tabby?" Autumn questioned as she walked next to Leland.

"Tabitha's husband, Mason, is the State Fire Marshal. We have known them forever, and since Sierra came to terms with her little side, the three of them have become really close," Leland replied. "I assume she told you she was a little when you told her we were dating?"

Autumn nodded. "I have known she was a little for a long time. I chose to keep it quiet until she decided she wanted me to know."

"She has struggled with that side of herself for a long time. Hell, she still fights it a lot of the time, but Tabitha and Mason have helped tremendously."

As they stepped out onto the deck, Autumn nodded toward the tall man who stood as far away from Sierra and Tabitha as he could get while still being on the deck. "Why is Zander so obviously ignoring them? And what is with the dirty looks?"

Anger was evident in Leland's voice when he replied, "Zander was Sierra's Daddy Dom until about two months ago, when he told her it was him or them. Meaning Tabby and Mason. When Sierra refused to choose, he broke it off with her."

"But if she isn't having sex with them, what does it matter?"

Leland shrugged. "I don't know. Mason and Tabby live a few hours away, so when they come to town, Sierra spends as much time with them as she can. The only reason I can think of for him to be that way is that Zander doesn't like to share, so when the jealousy got to be too much for him, he lashed out and gave her the ultimatum. Sierra refused to give up people she thought of as family just because his green-eyed monster was rearing its ugly head."

"So rather than share her non-sexually on the occasional weekend visit, he broke up with her? He's an idiot."

"Agreed." Leland nodded as he stopped a few feet away from the other people on the deck. "The plan for the night is to sit around a fire and shoot the shit, but I need for you to let me know if you are uncomfortable with anything. It does not mean I will change or stop what is happening, but I will explain it and attempt to reassure you. If you are still overwhelmed, we will find a quiet place inside to discuss the issue."

Autumn smiled up at him. "I trust you and your judgment to keep me safe both physically and emotionally."

"Are you sure you want to trust him? He seems pretty shady," a woman teased from behind Autumn.

Autumn was thrilled when she turned around to respond and saw who was asking the question. "Liv! Oh, my gosh! What are you doing here?" Liv glanced at her toes for a few seconds before she reached for the man who was talking to another couple a few feet away. When he turned around, Autumn was shocked. "Chief?"

"We are here because my husband is very good friends with the host, and it's nice to start on the right foot when it comes to new neighbors," Liv shared as her eyes shifted about the yard in an attempt to look anywhere but at Autumn.

"New neighbor? You guys live across the road? So, you sold Lee the house?"

"Yeah."

"Wait." Autumn paused, her brain had finally caught up with the conversation. "You're married to Kevin? My boss?"

Liv at least had the courtesy to look sheepish when confronted with the truth. She tucked a strand of her shoulder-length, black hair behind her ear as her husband wrapped his arms around her middle in a show of support. "I didn't think it was a big deal when you and I first started talking. By the time I realized I should have told you, we had become close, and I didn't want you to think I had been deceitful. I didn't want to wreck our friendship."

Autumn looked from Liv to the chief—no, Kevin—a few times. She was about six inches shorter than her husband's six-foot frame, fitting perfectly under the crock of his arm. "Tell me you kept all the names I call him to yourself."

Liv gathered Autumn in her arms as soon as she finished talking. "I may have told him a few things, but it was absolutely no fault of my own. He is extremely persuasive when holding a looped belt in his hand."

"My personal favorite was when you called me a 'reflective vest Nazi.'"

Autumn groaned as she pushed her friend away to give her a phony dirty look. "Liv! I called him that just last week!"

"Sorry, but he knew you would have something to say after your written warning from the car crash, and as I said, he wields a mean strap." She reached back to rub her bottom with a pout on her face in an attempt to gain sympathy.

"I know you too well, Liv." Autumn laughed. "You dangled

that information in front of him and withheld it until you got what you wanted. You forget how much we've shared, which kind of makes me wonder how you kept who you were married to from me for over a year." Autumn shook her head. "But that is *not* the point. The point is that I know how much you love it when he uses leather on your ass, and I know he only ever uses it in play because it is not much of a deterrent for you."

"Good try, love, but she has your number," Kevin teased his wife before kissing the top of her head.

"You can't blame a girl for using every advantage she had."

"Your advantage is officially cut off. From now on, I will swear you to secrecy before I tell you anything!"

Leland butted in on the conversation before Liv could get a retort in. "Hello, Nurse Liv."

Liv blushed a pretty shade of red as her eyes narrowed slightly. "Are you guys ever going quit calling me that?"

"Absolutely not," her husband declared as she turned to him and ran her fingers through the speckling of gray hairs at his temple.

Autumn stared at Leland. "Why would you tease her about being a nurse?"

"Oh, we aren't teasing her for being a nurse. We are teasing her because when she is in nurse mode, she is anything but submissive. To anyone."

"A few years ago, when Leland was here for a visit, Olivia had to work a 12-hour shift. As soon as she strolled in the door after work, she started barking orders at the two of us like it was nothing."

"I never barked orders."

"Yeah, you do," Leland interjected, an amused smile on his face as he reached back to rub his head. "You even whacked the back of my head when I didn't move my boots off your coffee table quick enough."

"You guys exaggerate this story more and more every time you tell it."

Giving his sulking wife an amused look, Kevin continued. "When I relieved her of her scrubs and pulled her across my lap for her well-deserved punishment, she had the audacity to lay naked over my lap and blame the whole thing on 'Nurse Liv.' I laughed so hard I nearly forgot to blister her hide. Nearly."

"From what I have seen, if a nurse is submissive at work, she gets stomped all over and ends up hating her job. She doesn't have a switch she can flip as soon as she gets home that takes her from work mode to wife mode in the blink of an eye."

"No, there is no switch." Kevin smirked when he heard the groan from his wife. "But making her take off her scrubs in the garage before she is allowed into the house is an *excellent* way to get her into her submissive mindset when she comes home."

In a cheeky gesture, Liv stuck her tongue out at her husband. As soon as she saw the look on his face, she sucked her tongue back into her mouth.

Kevin grabbed Olivia's elbow just as she started to backpedal. "Where are you going, girl?"

The fact that the question was directed at someone else made no difference to Autumn; her stomach still fell to her toes at the sound of his deep, gravelly voice. Leland pulled her into his arms and anchored her in, giving her no choice but to stay put. "Don't you worry, subbie. They have been together a long time. She knew sticking her tongue out at her Dom would be an unwise decision."

"I'm sorry, Sir." Olivia's eyes dropped to the floor, but only for a second before her Dom grasped her chin and forced her eyes to connect with his.

"Are you allowed to be cheeky with me, Olivia?"

"Not while I am wearing your collar, Sir."

"Is it on that beautiful neck of yours?" He traced the beautiful gold chain in question with his index finger.

"Yes, Sir, I'm wearing it, just like you told me to."

"And what are the rules when you are wearing my collar and we are with people we love and respect?"

"I am allowed to be myself, but I must still be respectful, Sir."

Kevin clicked his tongue against the back of his teeth in a disapproving manner before he stuck his hand into his pocket and pulled out two clothespins.

"No, Master, please!"

"Laying it on a bit thick with the Master, aren't we, pet?" Kevin teased, even though a spark in his eyes gave away his appreciation of her efforts. "Oh, don't act surprised. You know what happens when my girl gets cheeky at the wrong time. My expectations for this relationship have never changed, love."

"But, Sir, I—"

"You didn't know I kept them on me? Of course not. I have to keep a few tricks up my sleeves or, rather, in my pocket." Kevin held out his hand with the clothespins in his palm. One had a yellow dot on the end while the other had a red dot. "What will it be? Are you going to wear the mean one on your tongue for four minutes? Or are you going with the yellow one for ten?"

"Please don't make me choose, Sir," Olivia pled as she did a nervous little dance in place, her elbow still held in the man's firm grasp.

"But making you choose your punishment is half the fun. Red or yellow?"

"Sir, please."

Kevin's voice lost all its previous playfulness. "Forcing me to repeat myself again would be ill-advised, sub. Red or yellow?"

"Yellow, Sir."

The stern man ran his hand down his wife's face in a soothing motion before he stuffed the red clothespin back into his pocket. He grabbed a thick, green cushion from a nearby chair and tossed it on the ground next to his feet. "Kneel, pet." Olivia gracefully knelt on the cushion with her butt resting on her feet and her knees spread slightly wider than shoulder width apart.

Autumn watched as Kevin knelt in front of his wife and had a quiet, private conversation with her. "Why are we standing here watching this like a couple of voyeurs? Shouldn't we be giving them some privacy?"

"If they needed or wanted privacy for this, he would have found some, but the knowledge and the embarrassment of knowing her friends are standing here watching the exchange between the two of them is part of her punishment. Now, sh. While we will watch their scene, we will not interrupt it by talking."

"Stick out your tongue," Kevin commanded, already holding the clothespin open in front of his wife's face. After a quick glance at the people observing the scene, Liv lowered her eyes and slowly obeyed. Her husband gently clipped the offending object into place before he spoke again. "You are to stay in position until I come get you. To answer the question I know is tumbling around in that pretty little head of yours, no, you are not allowed to move, so you can wipe away the drool that we both know will soon be dripping down your chin. You chose to be sassy, so you deal with the consequences. Ten minutes, love."

To Autumn's horror, Kevin straightened from his kneeling position and walked into the kitchen. "He is just going to leave her there with no way of knowing if she is okay? No protection?"

"Autumn, this is not a club." He turned her to face the rest of the people milling around the backyard. "This is a group of friends who all trust and know each other exceptionally well. Look around, what do you see?"

"A bunch of people lost in their own conversations."

Autumn jumped when his hand landed on her ass. "Try again. Look closer."

Autumn reluctantly did as she was told, and after a few seconds, his point became clear. "You're right. No one ever glances away from her for very long. They are all watching her, making sure she is all right."

"We have known each other a long time. Kevin, as a fire-fighter, trusts us all with his life, but more importantly, as a Dom, he trusts us with his sub." Autumn turned to the woman who still knelt on the cushion, a trail of drool making its way down her chin. "Part of her punishment is that her Dom is not standing at her side, but she knows he would never leave her unprotected. If she were not so lost in her submission, she would see what I do."

Autumn's gaze followed Leland's eyes to the open patio door. There, with a glass of water in his hand, leaning against the doorframe, was Kevin, his eyes glued to his wife. "She thinks he is ignoring her, but in truth, she has *all* his attention and more."

"I know you are not used to seeing scenes outside a club setting, but there is no need to worry. We all practice caution, and we don't subject our subs to anything they cannot handle."

"Will we eventually do stuff like this?"

"Absolutely. You become disrespectful or break any of our rules while we are someplace semi-private like this with people we trust, and I will not hesitate in the slightest to remind you of your place."

Autumn turned around again and spoke into Leland's chest. "Thank you for making me watch and helping me to understand that a scene in a private setting like this could be so different yet so much like a scene at a club."

Leland smiled down at her after placing a kiss on the crown of her head. "That is my job as your Dom."

The single high-pitched beep caught Autumn's attention a few minutes later, and she turned to watch Kevin cross the deck. He knelt in front of his wife and spoke for a few seconds before removing the clothespin from her tongue. He gave her a drink of water and wiped her chin with a paper towel.

"I'm sorry, Sir," Liv said as her husband scooped her into his arms and carried her to an out of the way chair.

"Come on, princess, let's give them some time. When she is ready, they will rejoin the group. How about a drink?"

"Morgan and Coke, please," she said as they entered the kitchen. She moved to the cupboard and grabbed the biggest glass she could find.

"Whoa, pet, you are not using that colossal glass."

The sass dripped from Autumn's every word. "You said I could have *one* drink. You never said what size of glass that *one* drink had to be in, and this is the glass I choose."

Leland's eyebrows rose, and a crease formed between them even as a smile threatened to form on his lips. "That loophole is not going to work. Yes, I said you could only have one drink. No, I did not specify what size of the cup you were to use, but this is me telling you now that you will not use that cup."

Autumn realized as soon as she finished rolling her eyes at the maddening man that it was an unwise move. He instantly went from playful boyfriend to annoyed Dom, and when she saw him reach for the drawer that held the kitchen utensils, the apologies fell from her mouth. "I'm sorry, Sir. I didn't mean to. They just rolled."

"Now, pet, an apology should never be followed by an excuse." He pulled a wooden spoon from the drawer before he strode over to the sliding glass door that separated the two of them from the rest of the people and flipped the lock. "I am offering you some privacy this time because I know you are not ready to be on display in front of your coworkers, but know this... this will be the only time you are allowed this luxury."

"Sir, I—" Her plea was cut short by the sound of the spoon landing sharply upon Leland's thigh.

"Shit! Okay, so not that hard," he mumbled to himself as he rubbed his leg to alleviate the sting caused by his self-inflicted swat. He tested the implement once more, and obviously happy with it, he turned back to Autumn. "Turn around. Shorts and panties down. Hands on the counter. Butt out. This is also the only time I will allow you any privacy when baring yourself for punishment. Say 'thank you, Sir' and do as I ask, please."

"Thank you, Sir," Autumn croaked before she turned to face the counter. Her hands shook as she tried to work the button from its tight hole. She was not scared but nervous. This was the first time Leland had actually gone through the whole production of disciplining her. She knew the few random swats before then were going to be nothing like what she was in for in a few short moments. *If she could ever get her damn shorts down.*

Finally, the button slipped free, and the zipper slid down easily. She pushed her thumbs into the side of her shorts, and taking a wobbly breath, she shoved them past her hips so they could pool around her ankles. Her lacy pale blue boy shorts quickly joined the pile of fabric tangled at her feet. She had attempted and failed a deep calming breath before she grasped the edge of the counter.

"Bottom out," Leland commanded as he rubbed his hand up and down her back in a soothing manner. "Your hands are to stay on the counter, understand? I do not want to have to worry about hitting your fingers. Your ass can take this punishment without any lasting damage; your fingers cannot." As soon as he finished talking and received the required answer from Autumn, he shifted to her left side and placed the spoon on her bottom. The smooth wood was drawn across her skin in small circles. When he lifted the spoon in preparation for the first strike, she jumped. "Easy, pet. I haven't started yet."

Just as Autumn relaxed and let out a lungful of air, the spoon bounced off her left cheek. "Ow! Son of a—"

"Don't you dare finish that statement," Leland scolded without letting up on his back and forth assault on her bottom. "I do not appreciate swearing from my sub in everyday conversation, so I would discourage cursing while you are already in trouble and I have you in such a prime position to correct that unwise choice."

It didn't take long for Autumn to wiggle and dance in place, trying to alleviate some of the stinging pain the horrid wooden implement left in its wake. She realized quickly that rising up on her toes in an attempt to get away from his relentless assault on her posterior was a foolish idea. It was no skin off his nose if his swats landed on the well-padded curve of her bottom or the tender crease where her thighs met her globes. However, it only took one spank to her delicate sit spot for her to decide it mattered to her very much. "Oh, my God!" she wailed as she planted her feet flat on the floor.

"If you would have stayed still, my spoon would have landed where I intended. Doesn't feel too good when you move and I miss my mark does it, princess?"

"No, Sir," Autumn cried just as he switched up the rhythm, causing her to lose track of where he would strike next. "I'm sorry, Sir! I won't roll my eyes again. I promise!"

When his assault on her backside continued, she gave in to her fate and rested her head on the counter, her resistance all but spanked out of her. He landed about a dozen more before she heard the spoon clatter to the floor and she was turned and gathered in Leland's arms. That was when the dam holding her emotions at bay broke. "I'm sorry I rolled my eyes, Sir, and that I'm such a blubbering mess."

"A few tears never hurt anyone. You're okay, princess. Just let me hold you."

Chapter 6

"**E**veryone is staring at me," Autumn complained as the couple rejoined the people on the deck.

"They are not staring at you. In fact, everyone is being extremely polite and acting like they didn't just hear every swat and resulting squeal as my favorite spanking spoon met your ass repeatedly." Autumn's stopped in her tracks, and her mouth dropped open at his bluntness.

"You'd better shut your mouth before he decides to put it to good use," Sierra cautioned as she ran past them and into the house.

"She is not kidding," Tabitha teased as she pushed on the bottom of Autumn's chin, gently pushing her jaw shut. She smiled at Leland as she continued. "He has done it before, many times. Bitten a few times for his efforts if I recall correctly."

Tabitha was a thin, tall woman, but her small frame clearly held strength and confidence. Her long hair was a dirty blonde color, and the lines starting to form at the corners of her eyes showed she was quick to smile. Autumn instantly liked her.

A chill visibly ran through Leland's body before he spoke. "I am not going to validate that comment with a response. I am guessing that you are taking my little sister with you later tonight?"

"That was what I was coming over to tell you. She has convinced me to let her have one s'more before we leave, but as soon as she is done burning her marshmallow to a crisp, we are leaving for her apartment. I haven't told her yet, but Mason's plane lands here at six tomorrow morning, and we are going to pick him up."

"Didn't want to pick up the grouchy old man by yourself, did you?"

"Of course not! That man hates traveling, and having her with me will save me from His Almighty Grumpiness. For a while anyway."

Leland laughed. "Good luck with that. She will shove you at him in a second in order to save herself, and you know it. You also know you don't have to tell me you are taking my sister with you, right?"

"Of course, I have to tell you. She is your little sister, and after the last time she snuck away, I am not taking any chances."

Just then, a blonde with two high pigtails and a huge, obnoxiously bright tutu around her waist trotted up the stairs directly to Zander. As soon as she was within arm's reach, he grabbed her waist and lifted her high above his head before turning his back to the crowd and settling her on top of the railing with her arms wrapped around his neck. The maneuver was clearly an exaggerated display of happiness. "I missed you, Papa!"

Leland turned to Tabitha with a meaningful expression on his face. Whatever he was trying to communicate to her was not shared quickly enough because as soon as Tabitha turned to go inside, Sierra skipped out to the deck, stopping suddenly when her eyes landed on the new arrival.

The strangled, "Daddy," that slipped from Sierra's lips forced Autumn's stomach to drop to her toes; she was at her friend's side and had her gathered in her arms before anyone else moved.

When Sierra crumpled to her knees, Autumn went with her, impervious to the pressure the new position put on her sore bottom. Her friend needed her.

They were a crumpled heap of body parts for only a few seconds before Leland untangled the two of them, slipped his arms under his sister and carried her back into the house. Tabitha rushed past her, leaving Autumn where she was.

"Go with them," Kevin said as he helped her from the ground and gave her a nudge toward the door.

"But they have it handled. They will help her." Uncertainty welled up inside her.

"Sub, I am telling you to go with them. Sierra is not the only one who needs a little extra strength right now."

A glance toward Liv gave her the reassurance she had needed before she did as Kevin directed. When she finally reached the living room, Sierra was on the sofa next to Tabitha, her head in the older woman's lap.

"Why? He said he loved me!"

"I am going to kick his ass," Leland growled as he stomped toward the door.

Autumn had to sprint to cut him off before he got outside and did exactly as he said he would. "Leland, you can't do that!" She tried to reason with the protective big brother in front of her, even as the need to scream at Zander and scratch the unknown woman's eyes out settled like a stone in the pit of her stomach.

"I am not going to let that douchebag be an asshole and break my sister's heart. Fire brother or not, my fist is going to meet his face. Move, sub." He actually growled at her, his voice the deepest she had ever heard. When she didn't do as he demanded, he seized her waist, physically picked her up and moved her to the side before attempting to storm past her.

She went to her tiptoes and grasped the collar of his shirt as tightly as she could, refusing to let go. The glare he shot her way should have killed her on the spot, but she pushed forward. "She loves him, Lee, and if you go out there swinging, you are not going to accomplish anything. She will only resent you for hurting him. Sierra does not need you to beat up every guy who breaks her heart; she needs you to help comfort her."

Leland visibly deflated then rubbed his hand across his face and pried Autumn's fingers from his garment. "You made your point, princess. You can let go now." He planted a kiss on her lips before taking her hand and leading her back to living room. "Tabitha, I think you'd better let her in on your surprise."

"I don't want a surprise!"

"Not even a surprise that involves picking up Mason from the airport tomorrow?" Tabitha dangled the proverbial carrot in front of Sierra.

Sierra picked her head up from Tabitha's lap. "Mason? You said he was busy with work."

"Yes. I wasn't going to tell you until morning, but his plane gets in at six, and we are going to pick him up."

A repulsed expression crossed Sierra's face. "Six in the morning?"

"Afraid so."

Sierra groaned. "He is going to be *so* grouchy that early in the morning."

Everyone laughed as Tabitha helped the smaller woman off her lap and stood before taking her hand. "Let's go, lovely. We will both need a good night's sleep to deal with the bear in the morning."

Leland turned to Autumn. "I am going to escort them out. I saw that Kevin and Liv had rejoined the group. Go hang out with them and I will be there shortly." He softened his command with a kiss to her forehead as he turned to follow his sister out of the house.

Autumn navigated her way through the throng of people on the deck to the table where Liv and Kevin were sitting. "I told you that others were going to need your support and strength. Good job, sub."

"How did you know he would react that way?"

"I had hoped he wouldn't, but I know what it's like to have your little sister hurting and you can't do anything about it."

"I didn't think I would be able to stop him."

Kevin laughed. "We were ready for him out here. If you were unable to stop him, he would have been hog-tied before he got anywhere near Zander." Kevin tipped his head toward a man who was coiling up a length of rope.

"I would have paid to see that," Liv snorted as she tried unsuccessfully to hide her smile.

Chapter 7

"Meeting. Great room. Ten minutes," the chief ordered as he strode past Autumn and Liv, landing a hard swat on his wife's bottom as he went. "You. Go lie down in my office."

"Don't be silly."

Kevin turned around, continuing his journey backward. "You are about to fall asleep on your feet. Go lie down."

Liv laughed. "I am a nurse. The only way we know how to sleep is on our feet."

Kevin stopped dead in his tracks. "Are you arguing with me, sub?"

Olivia took a cautionary step back. "Sir?"

"Olivia."

"I wasn't. I didn't intend to actually disobey you. I was teasing."

In two steps, he had her in his arms. "I'm sorry, love. I know you're not trying to be difficult. There is some shit going on, and I took it out on you. I'm sorry." Liv winked at Autumn, clearly pleased with herself. "You *were* in the clear, but that was before you insinuated that you had me wrapped around your finger with that little wink of yours."

"How did you—" Olivia started.

"I have my ways. Now, march." He smacked her on the ass to get her moving and threw his comment over his shoulder as he followed his scampering wife. "Meeting in the great room. Fifteen minutes."

"Really, how did you know I winked at Autumn?" Olivia questioned as they ambled into the office.

"You just told me."

The last thing Autumn heard before the door to the office shut behind the couple was a grumble from Liv at the realization she had just ratted herself out set in.

"IS it just me or was that a really long ten minutes?" Zander harassed the chief as he strolled into the room twenty minutes later.

"What can I say? My wife needed me." Kevin allowed the men a few minutes of laughter at his expense then cleared his throat and called for order. "Okay, people, I am sure you are wondering why I called this meeting."

"And then forced us to wait."

"We have a situation." Any remaining jesting stopped dead as soon as the words registered. "As you may have noticed, we have had a good-sized fire every week for the past three weeks, and all of them have been on our shift. The fire marshal doesn't think it is a coincidence."

"How come?"

"Mason has received some letters. He didn't realize it at first because the letters started out as praising him for a job well done. Then he saw the pattern."

"A pattern?" one of the guys questioned from behind Autumn.

"Three days before every fire, he receives a letter. He didn't notice initially because the first one came the day after B shift had their car fire. He wrongly assumed that was the fire they were referring to. The second letter briefly referred to the lack of media coverage but continued the admiration of a job well done. The most recent letter was completely different. It seems our arsonist doesn't like that his work is being ignored for 'bigger' stories."

"That's dangerous," Leland commented before he put his elbows on his knees and his head in his hands.

"Exactly, which is why I called this meeting. I need each one of you to be on the alert. He or she is no longer content with just setting some vacant buildings on fire. The arsonist has threatened to move to residential buildings." The whispered moans of annoyance echoed through the room. "This is why I need you all on alert. They are going to beef up the police who are present at our scenes, but more units and flashing lights will draw more spectators, especially if he follows through on his threat to move to a residential area. We all know the profile of an arsonist. They do not start the fire and run. They almost always stay to watch the action play out. So, while you are being aware, let me or a PD unit know if you think you recognize someone from one of our past fires or see something out of place."

"When was the last time Mason got a letter?" Autumn questioned, fearing she already knew the answer to her question.

"Three days ago."

"Fuck." Autumn's curse joined the chorus of profanity from nearly everyone else in the room. The only difference was that no one else received a sharp pinch to the thigh when the person next to them heard the swear. When she jumped, some of the annoyed moans and grumbles turned into amused chuckles as it became apparent to those closest to the couple what had happened.

Leland leaned over to whisper in her ear, "You just earned yourself your first at work spanking. Congratulations."

"You are going to spank me for swearing when everyone else, including you, said and is feeling the same thing I am?" Her whispered reply was a little harsher than she intended.

"Watch the tone, and if you had said any word other than *that* word, I would have let it slide. I hate hearing that word, especially from your mouth."

"I ask you to fuck me all the time, and you have yet to whack me for that."

"You know that is different."

"If you two have finished squabbling," Kevin interjected, thankfully keeping Autumn from digging herself deeper.

Leland had the decency to blush for a second before a shit-eating grin split his handsome face in two. "Sorry, Chief."

"So we are going to have a fire tonight?"

"If he sticks with his pattern, yes." Autumn selected a different swear word to emphasize her emotions this time, and her reward was a tender squeeze of her knee. "If he continues to follow his pattern, then the fire will be called between the hours of midnight and four in the morning. So, get some sleep while you can and cross your fingers that he will change his mind about involving pedestrians. Dismissed."

Autumn was out of her seat in a second.

"Stop." Leland waited until his mouth was by her ear to give the next directions, "Kevin asked to talk to me after the meeting. I need you to go all the way to the back of the repair closet. Push past the last rack of bunkers, and there is some vacant space behind it. I want to find you there kneeling in front of the shelves. I will be there as soon as I'm done speaking with him. Go."

"Yes, Sir."

"Good girl." Who knew those two little words could put a smile on her face and make her belly flop?

When she swung the door to the repair closet open, the thick smell of smoke assaulted her senses. She stepped into the long room and started making her way to the back. The first half of the room was relatively organized. Bunker gear hung on hooks waiting to be fixed while SCBA replacement pieces lined the shelves, but that was where the organization ended. As soon as she passed the halfway mark, the floor became littered with every-thing imaginable. She found shattered facemasks, a broken frying pan, and even a boot with an ax blade embedded in the toe.

She navigated her way through the discarded equipment to the final row of old dusty bunker coats hung neatly in a line. She forced her way between a couple of the coats and stepped into the vacant space behind them.

The makeshift room was about the size of a large walk-in closet and void of nearly anything, especially when compared to the clutter on the other side of the coat wall. All the space contained was a dusty old bookshelf which, coincidentally, already had a cushion placed in front of it, and a couch that looked like it had been a recent addition. "Guess I am not the first sub to be sent here."

"You most certainly are not."

Autumn jumped. "Sir, I didn't hear you come in. I just got back here and was looking around before I got into position."

"Calm down, princess. My talk with Kevin didn't take as long as I thought it would. I expected you to take in your surroundings before you did as I directed. You're not in any more trouble than you already were."

"What did he want to talk about?"

He pointed at the cushion and only began to speak after she started to do as he bid. "He wanted to give me a heads-up. This lunatic has taken some interest in my sister."

She stopped cold in her tracks. "Sierra?"

"Yes. It appears he has deemed her the perfect new journalist to tell his story, and he has demanded she be the correspondent at all his fires. The police think that this is the best course of action."

"You're kidding?"

"Unfortunately, no. They believe this to be a small way they can keep him happy and, hopefully, keep him from upping his game in the process." Leland nodded his head toward her destination.

"She didn't agree to do this, right?" Autumn questioned as she sank to her knees on the plush square.

"Of course, she agreed. She has no problem putting herself in harm's way for a story, and she has no one to tell her no. No one she will actually listen to."

"You can. She will listen to you."

"She won't. She may accept my discipline from time to time when she believes she deserves it, but I am only her big brother. My opinion only carries so much weight."

"What about Tabby and Mason? They can tell her what a horrible idea this is. She will listen to them."

"Mason talked to her about it this weekend and got nowhere." When Autumn opened her mouth to argue, he held up a hand. "Enough. She already agreed to do it, so she can't back out. Now, if I were you, I would start worrying about yourself, sub."

The reminder of why they were there was like flipping the submissive switch. Her eyes instantly fell to the floor next to his feet. "Sorry, Sir."

"Why are we here, princess?"

Autumn swallowed hard before she met his eyes. "That's my issue, Sir. I don't agree with why we are here."

"Explain, please."

"Usually by this time in punishment, I'm at least a little remorseful, but this time is different. I am not sorry I swore."

"Why do you think this time is different?"

"I was in the middle of a heated situation. I had just been told that some lunatic is targeting our shift specifically. I don't believe I reacted inappropriately to the situation. However, I believe you did."

"You know how I feel about that word."

She looked at the pillow she knelt on. "I do, Sir, but fu— that word has become a habit. You cannot expect me to all of a sudden quit saying it. It is going to take time, practice, and—"

"Punishments." Leland finished her statement for her as he crouched in front of her, lifting her chin so he had her eyes. "I am not expecting perfection, princess, but I am expecting you to accept my assistance in helping you to remember our agreed upon rules and my hatred for the word when it comes from your beautiful lips. You need to accept my help, and if that help comes in the form of my hand or an implement being applied to your ass, then so be it. You agreed to this type of relationship, and unless you say your safe word, I am going to deal with you breaking our rules the way I see fit. The way we agreed it should happen." He paused, giving her a chance to tap out before he straightened and took a single step back. "Stand and bare yourself, please."

"Yes, Sir." Autumn felt her resistance melt away, the regret of her actions filling the void it left in its wake. She slid her pants and panties to her calves and felt the chilled air hit her heated sex.

He removed his radio from his hip and placed it on one of the shelves before he pushed the cushion to the middle of the room and placed a folded blanket in front of it. "Back on your knees, please. Forehead on the blanket. Ass in the air."

She did as she was told, and for a long while, Leland stood silently behind her. When her curiosity got to be too much, she spoke, "Sir?" As soon as she moved her head in an attempt to see him, his hand came down sharply on her upturned bottom.

"You are to stay in the position I put you in until you are given permission to move."

"Sorry, Sir! I won't move."

His pant leg brushed against her leg and raised goose bumps on her skin. "I am only going to use my hand. I don't want you to be too sore at work, but make no mistake, princess, we will be finishing this chat at my place tomorrow after shift. Is that clear?"

"Yes, Sir."

Her words were still ringing in her ears when the first smack landed. He was not attacking her derriere as vigorously as he usually did, and the fact he took into consideration where they were relaxed her the slightest bit as the rhythmic discipline was applied. The worry caused by the meeting melted away, taking with it the fear she had for her friend's safety. The sensation was euphoric even if it was only for a short time.

She was just starting to wiggle when she felt the first smack land on her sit spots, signaling that the chastisement would be coming to an end soon, at least for now. A sigh passed through her lips when, after ten on each tender area, Leland lifted her, took her place on the cushion and gathered her in his lap with her pants and underwear still around her calves.

They sat like that for a few minutes while he allowed Autumn to gather her bearings and, unknowingly, a bit of her sass, too. "I'm sorry I used the word you hate so much, even if I think it was a tiny bit justified in the given situation."

Leland clicked his tongue against the back of his teeth. "You are wearing my freshly placed handprints on your still bare ass because you let your mouth run without its filter, yet you still continue to sass without worry. Do you know how easy it would be to flip you over and give you another dose?"

She felt heat rush to her face. "I know, Sir, but I promised when we started this that I would be honest with you, and this is me being honest."

"I appreciate the honesty, princess, and I hope you appreciate the honesty of my displeasure when my paddle makes contact with this beautiful tush of yours in the morning." He gave her ass a sharp pinch that had her jumping in his lap before he helped her stand and right her clothes. "For now, I will allow it, but know this, sassy one... if you make me regret letting you have an IOU, then I will never take it easy on you again, even if we are at work. Understand?"

"Yes, Lee."

"HE STUCK WITH HIS PATTERN," Autumn grumbled early the next morning as she rode in the passenger seat of the rig.

"Looks that way," Gwen replied over the wail of the sirens from both the fire trucks in front of them and the ambulance itself.

Autumn pulled the laptop mounted on the dashboard a little closer to her lap. "According to dispatch, a homeless man was inside the abandoned building when it started and had some minor burns to his arm. He states he was the only one inside the old library at the time."

She finished talking as they pulled up to the scene. The ancient brick building had flames curling from every one of the visible windows. A small group of men huddled around a soot-covered man on the grass in front of the building. Autumn jumped from the rig, grabbing the bag from the back before her partner turned the rig around and parked it in front of some hedges in case they had to leave quickly. She pushed past the fire-fighters who surrounded the slightly confused gentleman and listened to his lungs before introducing herself. "Sir, my name is Autumn. Can you tell me what happened?"

Autumn listen to him ramble off what dispatch had already told her as she handed her partner a bottle of sterile saline to pour over the burn on the man's arm. "Lungs sound good, and there is no soot around his nose or mouth," she shared as she shoved the stethoscope in the bag and stood.

"The burning on his arm is very minor."

"Good. I will get the cot so we can get him loaded into the rig." She jogged back to the ambulance and threw open the back doors. "Who the hell put this in here?" she called out in disgust as she picked up the charred piece of red fabric that lay on top of the previously pristine cot. As the fabric unfolded in her gloved hands, she realized what it was. "Chief!" Her cry drew more attention than she intended, and in a matter of seconds, she was surrounded by three men in bunker gear.

"What's wrong?" Leland questioned as he pushed the brim of his helmet back so she could make out who he was.

"This was crumpled up in the rig. When we left the station, nothing was back here. I instinctively check the back of the rig every time we go on a call. He had to have put it here."

"Is that our flag?" Jensen questioned as he tipped his head to the side to get a better look.

"Not *ours* but a duplicate, yes," Chief Atwood confirmed before talking into his radio. "Dispatch, how far out are those PD units?"

"Our closest unit is two minutes out."

"Copy that. Can you make sure an officer comes to the bus we have on scene as soon as they arrive? We have a situation."

"Ten-four."

Kevin's arm fell from his mic as he turned back to the group. "He is apparently here. I want eyes open and everyone on red alert. Keep doing your job, but make sure you are careful. No one else needs to know about the flag. If anyone questions why we are on red alert, say the cops think he is here. If this is an inside job, I want this kept as tight lipped as possible."

"Wait... you think this is an inside job?" Jensen questioned.

"They haven't ruled it out yet." An officer joined them as the chief finished his whispered reply.

"What do we got?"

"Singed flag was found in the back of the rig. Autumn is the only one who has touched it, and she did so before she realized what it was. She also says it was not in the ambulance when they left the firehouse. The arsonist has to be here," Chief answered as the flag was put into a big zipper top bag and sealed with red tape.

"I will let the guys know the perp may be in the vicinity, but I want radio silence about this. There is no reason to give him a heads-up if he is here," the officer ordered before he jogged to join the newly arrived officers.

A thuddy, painless swat landed on Autumn's butt. "Get your patient and get out of here, princess. We will see you back at the station."

Chapter 8

"**D**id you get any sleep after the call?" Autumn questioned as they pulled into Leland's garage later that morning.

"No, a few of us were in the meeting with PD until about thirty minutes before the end of the shift."

"Oh, Lee. Why don't you go climb into bed?"

The bark of laughter that escaped from Leland instantly told her that her plan was dead in the water. "Don't think so, princess. You are owed a paddling, and I am not about to let you convince me otherwise. In fact, with how tired you usually are after I'm finished with your ass, it is pretty much guaranteed that I will have a warm body to cuddle with when I do go to sleep. Right after I set that ass of yours on fire."

A broad smile spread across her face. "Well, it was worth a shot," she said before she swung her door open and ran into the house as fast as her legs would carry her.

His footfalls sounded loudly behind her as he ate up the distance with his long legs. "I will catch you, Autumn, and when I do, your ass is mine."

"You have to catch me first!" As soon as she got the words out of her mouth, he grabbed her around the waist, and she was sailing through the air as he sat on the foot of the bed. She landed with a grunt across his knees, ass exactly where he wanted her.

"No," she cried out at his hand came down on her canvas covered butt.

"Oh, yes, princess." Leland chuckled as he brought his hand down a few more times. Then he stood with Autumn tucked under his arm and stalked to his side of the bed where he sat once more. He stood her on her feet in front of him. "You didn't plan your escape route very well, girl. You not only trapped yourself in a dead end but also led me right to some of my favorite implements."

Autumn pushed her unruly, brown hair out of her face as he pulled open the bottom drawer of his nightstand. As soon as she saw the copious amount of implements it held, she started talking. "I won't ever use the f-word again. I promise, Sir."

"I don't believe that for a second, princess. You said, yourself, that it would be a difficult habit to break. What I do believe is that you will think twice for a while before you use that word again." He reached into the drawer and shifted the items around as if searching for something specific. "What should I use to teach my princess my hatred for this word? Let's see. We have a Ping-Pong paddle, no. I could use the strap, but I promised her a paddling. Oh, here it is!" He pulled out an older, wooden hairbrush. "This is my mom's. I hid it from her when I was a kid so she couldn't tan *my* hide with it. Found it in one of my old boxes when I moved in. I think we will use this."

Autumn squeaked when he grasped the front snap of her cargo pants. "I... do, do we have to start bare, Sir?"

"Of course, we do." When she opened her mouth to speak again, he talked over her. "Are you arguing with me?"

"But we haven't." She blushed and looked away.

"Eyes on me, princess. Good girl. Now, tell me why this is any different than the other times I have spanked this beautiful ass of yours. Do you still believe this is an unjust punishment?" He cupped her chin when she tried to look away again. "Talk to me."

"No, I deserve it. I just." The fire in her eyes grew as she struggled to speak, and when she finally did, the words were less than respectful. "We haven't had sex yet, okay? And you're going to see everything!"

Before she knew what was happening, she was sitting on Leland's lap, her head tucked under his chin and a sense of right-ness settled over her. "You are worried about me seeing your pussy."

Autumn knew it wasn't a question, but she felt the need to explain. "Well, yeah. You said you liked your girl's pussy bare, and I am far from bare. I haven't had time to get waxed, and I can't shave because the ingrown hairs hurt so badly. If you see it now, you are going to be disappointed because it isn't the way you want it and—"

The rest of Autumn's words were an unintelligible mumble as Leland covered her mouth with his hand. When she finally stopped talking, he spoke. "I think you are making excuses because you are nervous, and not about the paddling you have coming. Right?"

"Maybe," Autumn whispered, not truly knowing the whole truth.

"You have no reason to be scared. Will I see your pussy? Yes, but I have seen glimpses of it before, when I have spanked you in the past. I am a gentleman. When we have sex is completely up to you."

Leland wrapped his arms tighter around her middle and gently started to rock her. They sat in the silence for a long while before Autumn took a deep breath and stood before him. "I think I'm ready now, Sir."

"Good girl, princess."

His praise settled deep within her chest, and a smile tipped up the corner of her mouth as she felt him take hold of the clasp of her uniform pants once more. Unsnapping them, he worked them down her legs and steadied her as she toed off her boots and stepped out of the discarded clothing. She glanced down the front of her body. Her shirt ended right where her panties started so it would provide no coverage for her core.

"Ready?" Leland questioned as he rested his hands on her hips, waiting for her to give him the go ahead.

"I trust you, Sir, and I should have realized that before I had a mini hissy fit."

With a chuckle, Leland hooked his thumbs into the side of her panties and let them fall to the floor, leaving her in only her navy work shirt. "Why are you about to get paddled, princess?"

"I used the f-word, Sir. I know you don't like it, and I agreed to refrain from using it, but I used it anyway."

"Exactly." He effortlessly pulled her over his knees, letting her head and chest rest on the bed.

With her firmly tucked into his side, Leland wasted no time in starting her warm-up. His massive left hand bounced from one cheek to the next, turning her previously creamy bottom a beautiful shade of pink. As soon as she started to wiggle in discomfort, he stopped and picked up the hairbrush.

"Relax your ass, Autumn."

"I'm trying, but that is easier said than done, Sir."

"Good girl."

As soon as the words were out of his mouth, the hairbrush connected with its target. He got two more swats in before she was able to drag in enough breath to voice her opinion of the brush. "Ow! No more! No more!" He ignored her demands and continued his work. He was a master at keeping her on her toes. She never knew where the next swat would land, or if he would decide to be particularly evil and land a couple in the same spot, one on top of the other. "Oww!"

"It's a stinger, isn't it? I used to hate this thing, but now I have a nice appreciation for it." The only response Autumn had for him was a wail of pain as the brush moved from her butt to her upper thighs.

The assault on her legs only lasted a short while, but it was enough to get her to reach back in an attempt to save her poor, scorched skin. "Reaching back is never allowed, princess." He landed another hard spank to each delicate area before he moved back to her butt. "Are you going to be able to keep your hands out of my way, or do you need me to hold them for you?"

Autumn replied by taking hold of his wrist. When his long, calloused fingers wrapped around her own wrist, she relaxed over his lap. There was something about knowing he wasn't going to let her jeopardize her well-being again, even if it was just a few fingers, allowed her to slip deeper into her submission.

"Ready to finish this? Use your words. A shake of your head does not work here. I have to hear you say it."

"Yes, Sir, I am ready."

"Last ten. These are going to be the worst," he warned as he shifted her closer to his side, holding her a little bit tighter.

A little voice in Autumn's head told her that the added physical restraint should worry her, but the submissive in her overruled it, and she felt herself slip into her role a little more. However, when she felt the impact of the brush, her submissive voice disappeared, and the other voice snidely chanted 'I told you so.' Autumn screamed and tried desperately to escape the hold Leland had on her, but to no avail. Along with the strength of Leland's swats came speed. The last ten were applied rapidly, and before she thought it was possible, Autumn heard the sound of the brush being thrown back into the drawer.

Leland lay on the bed beside her and effortlessly pulled her into the crook of his arm, her head resting on his shoulder. He was quiet as he ran his finger through her hair as she cried, allowing her the time she needed to calm herself down. "A few tears never hurt anyone, princess. Let it out."

AUTUMN ROLLED onto her back and woke with a start. "Shit," she whispered as she rolled onto her belly and soothingly rubbed her ass before she stole a glance at the sleeping man beside her. Another stolen glance at the clock told her they had been asleep for only forty-five minutes, not long enough, but she knew sleep wasn't going to come. She was turned on, and until that was taken care of, awake, she would stay.

She bit her lip. She had a couple of options. She could take care of it herself. As if he knew what she was thinking, the man next to her rolled over and placed his hand on her tender bottom. Yeah, that was out of the question. He would be upset if he woke up to find her playing with "his pussy," and her bottom could not take another spanking.

Option two, she could wait it out. Eventually, it would fade away, right? Autumn shifted, rubbing her thighs together just the tiniest bit. The flexing of her glutes causing Leland's hand to slip lower until his finger rested on the slit of her sex. Yeah, that choice wasn't an option, either.

That left only one thing to do. Jump his bones. Okay, not really, but it sounded like a good idea, and his manhood was already tenting the covers. She had to at least attempt to be submissive in the endeavor to get Leland to have his way with her, so step one, get permission.

Autumn wiggled closer to his naked body. *When did that happen?* she thought to herself right before she gave herself a slight shake and focused once more.

With her lips next to his ear, she asked in what she hoped to be her best bedroom voice, "Sir, may I suck on your cock?" As an afterthought, she sucked his lobe into her mouth and nipped at it softly.

The words may have gotten her nowhere, but sucking on his ear got her a yes. Sort of. His penis bobbed beneath the covers. That was as good a yes as any, right?

Not wanting to take any chances, she spoke to him again. "Sir, if your answer is yes, make your dick jump again." She watched the tent in the blankets as she took his earlobe in her mouth once more. She sucked harder this time. A smile spread across her face as she watched his penis jerk to life.

A hiss passed Autumn's lips as she sat up. As she made sure her butt didn't make contact with the bed, she stripped off her shirt and bra. As soon as she was as naked as he was, she dove under the covers, slid his legs apart and settled between them. For a few moments, she just looked at it. She had seen it before, through the shower curtain and such, but never this close, so she would take her time.

"If you stare at it much longer, princess, you are going to give me a complex," a sleepy Leland rumbled, causing her to jump. He threw the covers back, revealing Autumn in all her naked glory as she ogled his bobbing shaft.

"Were you faking this whole time?"

"Only since the first time you sucked on my ear."

"So pretty much the whole time?"

"Yes, princess, but now, because you elected to ask questions rather than put your lips to good use, you have lost the opportunity to have my cock in your mouth." Autumn's face fell, but Leland just chuckled. "Don't worry, sweetness, you will have my cock, but I can't wait any longer, so if you are ready for this step, it is going in your pussy." Autumn swallowed hard and eagerly nodded her head. "On your back."

A shriek escaped Autumn as she flopped onto her back, her butt connecting with the mattress, at the foot of the bed. "You want me on my back to torture me," Autumn pouted as she spread her legs eagerly for him.

"Just an added bonus, but I want to see the expression on your face when I slip my cock into you for the first time and then again when you scream my name as I make you come." Autumn blushed as she felt more cream coat her labia even though he hadn't even touched her yet. He grew serious, his face softening. "Are you ready?"

Autumn smiled evilly. "Do it already, before I take matters into my own hands." She moved her hand across her belly like she intended to do just that. Her hand didn't make it to her belly button before Leland landed a swat to her pussy.

"No topping from the bottom. You know you only touch this if I say you can, and I have not given you permission." Autumn watched as Leland grasped his manhood in his fist and inched closer to her core, rolling a condom in place. "We will discuss the need for condoms later, but right now, the patience required for that conversation has evaded me."

With that decree, they both watched as his cock disappeared inside her, her back arching more with every inch. The fullness rendered her speechless until he started slowly moving in and out. "I'm not going to break, Lee, Sir. I promise. Don't hold back."

His eyes closed briefly as he started pounding into her, his efforts bouncing the headboard against the wall. At that pace, it didn't take long for her nails for dig into his shoulder and her eyes to drift shut.

"Eyes on me, princess. I want you be looking at me when you ride my cock to oblivion for the first time."

His words were her undoing. Over the edge, she fell, and a wailed "Sir" slipped from her lips as her internal muscles clamped around the invading appendage. Leland went stiff for a few seconds then collapsed on top of Autumn as the tremors of his orgasm still wracked his body.

When he finally rolled off her, he gathered her in the crook of his arm once more. They were both sated and ready for sleep. Her tired eyes opened wide when Leland pinched her ass. "This is your warning, princess. Don't come without my permission again."

"Yes, Sir."

"And next time I tell you that you are going to scream my name, I don't want to hear 'Sir' bouncing off the walls. I want to hear my name fall from those lips. I want everyone within earshot to know that my girl is getting hers, and I don't want anyone to have to guess who is giving it to her. When I bring you to climax, you use my name. Got it, princess?"

A saucy smile curled up the corners of her lips. "Yes, Lee."

Chapter 9

Autumn rubbed her bottom as they crossed the gravel road to Kevin and Olivia's house. She had gotten a text from Liv asking if she was up for some gossip over a cup of coffee, and she had jumped out of bed at the opportunity. Well, right after Leland had let her up from round two.

It had been hours since Leland had taken that horrible, evil brush to her ass, but the deep ache was still there, reminding her of both his displeasure and love. It was the tenderness in her pussy that forced a smile to cross her face.

"Your smile makes me wonder if I should have landed a few more licks."

She stared up at Leland, thinking he had lost his mind. "More? Are you crazy? I am going to feel this for a couple of days as it is. I didn't need more."

They had walked through the garage and up to the door when he replied, "Then what is the smile for, princess?"

"I am enjoying my post-spanking soreness and my after-good-sex tenderness."

"You're enjoying your soreness? I definitely must not have paddled you hard enough."

It was a struggle to keep her eyes from rolling at his lame attempt to be funny. "Your wicked brush met my butt plenty, thank you very much. It was extremely effective. I'm just enjoying the afterglow of it all. That subtle soreness that lasts a few days, continually reminding me that you like me enough to correct me and not give up on us."

He stopped her from opening the door to the house with a hand on her shoulder. "You know I more than like you, right?"

"No, I don't know. You have never told me anything different." Without giving him a chance to respond, Autumn swung the door open and took a single step into the house before she stopped dead in her tracks at the sight before her. "Oh my gosh, I am so sorry!"

"Stop!" Kevin called as Autumn turned around to leave, pointing a thick, oak paddle at her.

"What do we have here?" Leland laughed as he spun Autumn around to face the kitchen. Imprisoning her in his arms, he forced her to stay put.

"What we have is a reason to knock next time we come over," Autumn declared as she attempted to cover her eyes with her hands, only to realize they were trapped at her sides by the hold Leland had on her.

"If you ever knock on my door, Autumn Rose, I will paddle you myself," Olivia called from her prone position, tears still sliding down her face.

Autumn gestured to Liv's current situation. She was bent over her kitchen table—her panties around her ankles, her jeans in a heap a few feet from her, her naked butt painted a brilliant shade of red. Her husband stood next to her with the thick, oak paddle in his hand. "You're joking, right? You are okay with us just wandering into your house in the middle of your punishment?"

Liv sniffed, wiping her face with her already damp sleeve. "I don't necessarily like it, but you are some of my closest friends, and I will be damned if one of my best friends is going to knock on my door!" She squealed when Kevin brought the paddle down harshly on her ass again. She gave him an apologetic look over her shoulder.

"Watch your mouth, sub."

"Sorry, Sir." She apologized before she turned back to Autumn and continued. "If you having free rein over my house puts us in weird positions at times, so be it. You guys practice the same lifestyle we do. Hell, you have seen Kevin punish me before."

"All I saw was your tongue, not your scarlet colored ass."

"Just like the last time, she knew mouthing off would end with her getting punished on the spot. Whether we had company coming over or not. Right, love?"

"Yes, Sir." Liv rested her forehead on her folded hands, seemingly ready to proceed with her punishment.

"Good, now let's finish this, please. As much as I would love to admire your beautiful behind all day, I have other, less important, things to attend to. Where were we, love?"

"We had just finished the 't' on the fifth set, Sir."

He wasted no time in bringing the implement down on his wife's bottom. He stared at her expectantly for a few seconds before he applied another swat. "Do we need to start all over, girl?"

"No! I mean. Please, Sir, don't start over. Please."

"Then I suggest you call out the letters as you are supposed to. The fact we have company does not excuse you from doing as you are told." The paddle quickly connected with its target two times.

"E! V!"

"You are kidding me," Autumn mumbled, realizing with those two letters exactly what had landed her friend in her current predicament.

"Don't interrupt, sub."

Her insides twisted before her stomach dropped to her toes at the growl she heard in Leland's voice right before he nipped at her earlobe and she started to melt into him.

"E!"

The cry from her friend prevented her from completely becoming a pile of goo at her man's feet. Reluctantly, she wiggled from his arms and walked around the table to stand across from her squirming friend, a you-should-have-known-better look directed at the prone woman.

"Figured out why she is here, did you?" Kevin questioned as he brought the implement down again, extracting the letter 'r' in the form of a squeal from his wife. "Whatever forever. Right, my love?"

"Yes, Sir."

"I thought she learned her lesson about this phrase the last time you got after her for it; she sure moaned about the punishment long enough for me to believe she had figured out that she needed to avoid that phrase at all costs. At the very least, I was sure she had learned not to use it when talking to you."

His laughter bounced off the walls. "My wife is a stubborn student. It takes more than a few lessons to get something through that thick skull of hers. Personally, I think she secretly loves the feel of my displeasure being applied to her ass via whatever implement I decide to use."

"Hey," Olivia whined pitifully from her still bent position. She turned back to scowl at her husband. "How come you can use the word whatever, but I get the paddle taken to me when I do?"

"Two reasons, love. I am the Dom, so I make the rules, and when I use that word, it is not said with a whine or accompanied by an eye roll or a foot stomp. It is said in its proper context, sans the attitude you always seem to inject into it." He brought the implement down again.

"I don't have any more letters, Sir!" Liv called out as she

raised on her toes, arched her back and looked at her friend for sympathy. Autumn just shook her head in answer to her friend's silent plea.

"That one was for the comma in your 'fine, whatever,' my dear."

"Thank you, Sir. I'm sorry you had to punish me."

A smile spread across Kevin's face. "Did my big, bad paddle chase my naughty, cheeky brat away?"

"For now, Sir."

He set the paddle down on the table. "Are you going to behave?"

Liv swallowed hard before she tore her eyes away from the most recent implement of torture and locked eyes with her husband. "I want to say I will be on my best behavior, Sir, but I'm not sure I can say that without it being a lie."

"Why is that?"

"Because I will never be perfect, Sir, and you were right."

"About what, love?"

"Even if I don't like them all that much when they are being applied, Sir, I still love the sensitivity your implements leave in their wake. Especially if you decide I need to feel your belt, Sir."

Kevin groaned painfully before he adjusted himself in his jeans. "You are an evil little subbie." He slapped her butt with the palm of his hand before he knelt behind her and took hold of her panties. Instead of pulling them up, he picked up her feet one at a time and physically helped her to step out of them. "Maybe the lack of panties and the touch of rough denim on your sore ass and bare pussy while having coffee with your friend will help to keep you in line." He retrieved her lost jeans and helped her into them before turning her from the table and pulling them over her battered bottom. As soon as they were snapped into place, Liv was wrapped tightly in her husband's arms.

Leland walked over to Autumn and wrapped his arms

around her from behind. She felt his breath brush against her ear as he whispered, "Seems to me, she enjoys the afterglow of a good hiding as much as you do." Autumn's snort forced a rumble of laughter from Leland's chest, and a smile spread across her face at the sound.

———————

"ARE we going to stand through coffee?"

Autumn turned from the field she was staring blankly at and took a sip from the mug she clutched in her hands. "Probably. If your rear end hurts half as much as it looked like it did, I doubt very much you are going to be willingly sitting anytime soon."

"Your backside hurts just as much as mine does."

Autumn tipped her head to the side before responding, "How do you know? I thought I was doing a pretty decent job of hiding it."

"Anyone who doesn't get their ass lit on fire on a regular basis would never have noticed, but you are talking to me. I am getting spanked, whether for punishment, play, or maintenance, at least three times a week. I saw the signs a mile away."

"Liar!" She paused for a second before reaching back to rub her still stinging nates. "Really? What gave it away?"

"You stood across from me while I was getting my 'just desserts' rather than sitting in the chair that was right next to you. Don't roll your eyes at me! A vanilla would never have noticed, but I am far from vanilla. More like cookie dough."

"You're more like paddle churned strawberry."

Liv curled her lip at her friend's lame joke. "You do know you don't have to hide this stuff from me, right?"

"I know." Autumn turned to the field again, took a sip from her mug, and continued. "I would have told you. I'm just a little off today."

"Because of the arsonist?"

"I am sure that has something to do with it." From the corner of her eye, she saw Liv step up beside her. "I just. On the way here, I thought Lee was going to say he loved me."

"That is awesome!"

"But I wouldn't let him."

"Do you love him?"

"Of course, I do. I wouldn't be wasting my time in this relationship if I didn't. I just think it's a little too early to be proclaiming it out loud to the man. I don't want to scare him off, and I want him to say it first." She dug the toe of her Converse into the dirt at her feet.

"But you wouldn't let him tell you?" Liv rolled her eyes. "Just tell him. If he loves you, he will say it back."

"And what if he doesn't love me back?"

"Is your ass sore?"

Autumn shot her friend an annoyed look. "You know it is."

"Then you know he loves you. He would not correct your behavior if he didn't. Now, whether he knows he loves you yet is another question. Men are dense like that. It usually takes them forever to interpret their emotions."

Autumn scuffed. "And if he isn't sure of his feelings, then what?"

"Then he will tell you."

"Why can't he just be a mind reader? Then he will just know how I feel without me actually having to tell him."

"Because those cuss words and sassy comebacks that float through your head would make it impossible for you to sit. Ever."

"I love the sound of my wife's laughter," Kevin said as he rounded the barn with Leland right behind him; both had motor oil smudges nearly to their elbows.

"Come give me a hug, woman," Leland demanded, his walk more like a stalk with every step he took toward the women.

"Leland." The word was drawn out as a warning as she set

her mug on the dirt next to Olivia's before they both started backing away from their filthy men.

"Kevin, keep your greasy hands to yourself," Olivia warned.

"Don't you think my greasy handprints would be an excellent addition to your red ass, love?"

"I know what you mean. Seeing my black handprints on Autumn's ass, one for each cheek," Leland groaned. "May be cause for round four."

"When was round three?" There was no way she could have stopped the smirk that curled her lips; she loved the playful side of her man.

"Round three will start when I lift you by your ass and take you against the barn. How else are my handprints going to get on that sexy pink butt of yours?"

"We have to make them work for it. It's more fun that way," Olivia whispered, her lips hardly moving.

"On the count of three, run. One."

"Two."

"Three!" Autumn took off as fast as she could toward the house.

"The chase is the best part." Leland chortled from way too close for her liking.

The sound of footfalls pounded behind her. She allowed him to get a few steps closer before veering toward the barn and narrowly escaping the arm that tried to encircle her waist. A quick glance back and Autumn had the satisfaction of seeing Leland's feet slide out from under him like he was sliding into home base, giving her the much-needed advantage. She dashed inside the barn and hurried into one of the stalls. She crouched against the wall and tucked herself as far into the corner as she could while she tried desperately to settle her labored breathing.

"I know you are in here."

Autumn regarded him through the gap in the boards as he

leaned against the barn wall without a care in the world. How was it that she was panting like a dog and he was completely unfazed by his pursuit of her?

"I'll tell you where she is if you go away without giving away my location," Olivia called from somewhere else in the barn.

"Hey!" Autumn exclaimed before slapping her hand over her mouth and holding her breath, fearing she had given herself away.

"So much for subbies united." Kevin laughed from the other end of the barn right before Liv let out a shriek. The sounds of Liv trying to escape her husband met Autumn's ears soon after. "You're mine now, sub."

"You have two choices, girl. You can either come out now and I will go easy on you, or you make me come find you."

Her stomach dropped to her toes as she swallowed a moan that threatened to further give away her hiding place. It took her all of half a second to decide she would stay exactly where she was. Olivia was right—being chased was half the fun, and if the noises coming from the other end of the barn were any indication, being caught was not all that bad, either.

"You took too long to decide, princess." His warm breath caressed her ear as the whispered words registered and forced a squeal of surprise to escape. His hand landed awkwardly on her ass. "Stand."

"No." She stubbornly sat down the rest of the way, wincing as her sore posterior took the majority of her weight.

A twinkle in his eye gave away the fact that he was enjoying this game as much as she was. "No?"

"Yes. I mean, no."

He tangled his hand in her hair, forcing her head back. "What is it? Yes or no, girl?"

"I said no, but the way your hand is tangled in my hair tells me that was not the response you were looking for. Sir."

"Damn right." He moved the hand holding her hair, forcing her to her knees. "Now, I have to show you what happens when you tell me 'no.' Hey, Kevin!"

"Yeah," Kevin yelled back, his voice tight.

"Want to help me teach my girl how to behave?"

"Only if you will help me with mine."

"My pleasure." His growl had Autumn's stomach in knots, and his tug on her hair had her on her feet. He leaned into her and took a deep breath before he spoke. "If this gets too intense for you, you have your safe word. You can stop this at any time."

"Are you going to share me?" Autumn was in no way okay with that scenario. Not yet.

"No, this time, we will keep our hands on our respective subs. Our eyes and comments should be enough to get the results we want."

"All right." She relaxed, releasing the breath she had unknowingly been holding. The only hands she needed or wanted on her were those of the man currently whispering in her ear.

"Your safe word is code."

"I know, Sir," she whispered back before she nipped sharply at his lobe. The sharp pain had him relaxing his grip on her hair, and she effortlessly slipped from his grasp.

However, she only got a few paces away before she was lifted off her feet. She fought the whole way across the barn, earning herself a heavy swat on her tender butt, which forced another shriek from between her lips. "Put me down you, you butthead!"

The men tried not to laugh, desperate to stay in the scene. Olivia had no such worries; she laughed so hard she snorted and had to lean on the waist-high bench that was behind her before she could speak again. "Did you just call him a butthead?"

"She got it from my sister," Leland shared as he placed her on her feet next to the other woman.

Liv smiled at her husband. "It does have a nice ring to it, doesn't it?"

"Don't even think about it, girl." Kevin's lip curled ever so slightly, reminding the women this was currently all part of a scene. No one was actually in trouble. They could put a halt to everything with one simple word. "Strip."

Autumn stood there for a second. Surely, she had misheard him. "Strip? Out here? Wait, you mean both of us?"

"City slickers." Leland shook his head like she was dense. "Yes, out here, and yes, both of you."

"But what if someone sees?"

"We are a fifteen-minute drive from the nearest town and the only people for miles. We are the only ones who will see your gorgeous, naked bodies."

Autumn grabbed the bottom of her shirt and looked at Liv. "He wasn't just telling me to strip, traitor. Offering to sell me out to keep your location a secret," she said in an overly exasperated tone as she pulled her shirt over her head in a swift movement before she toed off her shoes.

"All is fair in love and war, and you have to admit this was a bit of both." A smack landed on Liv's ass when she bent to remove her socks.

"Ha!" The gloat had hardly gotten passed Autumn's lips before her bottom received the same treatment. "Hey!"

"Princess, take those hands off your hips and continue stripping before I decide one swat was not enough."

With a pout firmly in place, Autumn did as he bid. Knowing he was a boob man, she deftly reached back and unhooked her bra, feeling their weight as she pulled the cups away from her chest. The sight of Leland adjusting his cock in his pants had her smiling as she reached for the button of her jeans, forcing her tits together a little more than they truly needed to be.

"Quit teasing me, or I swear to God." He grabbed her hair and forced her head back to expose her neck.

His lips suckled on her neck as she spoke. "But I thought that was the whole point of the game, Sir. You tease me, I tease you, and we both eventually win."

"She's got you there." Liv laughed as she pulled her shirt over her head, revealing that she only wore a shelf bra.

Taking his wife's nipple roughly between his thumb and pointer finger, Kevin spoke into the blissful face of his wife. "I suggest you get those jeans off quickly before I decide to cut them off your person. Leave the bra. It emphasizes you breasts impeccably."

"And as for you, my little tease, I think these lovely nipples of yours need a little bit of sparkle. Don't you agree?" Leland dug into his pocket and pulled out a pair of tweezer nipple clamps. Autumn's mouth dropped open.

"I see you are not the only one who keeps a few tricks in his pocket," Liv whispered to her husband as she straightened from removing her jeans, now completely naked apart from her bra.

"We may have made a detour before we met you girls in the yard."

"Cheaters!" both women accused at the same time.

"Forward thinkers," Leland corrected, taking Autumn's erect peak into his mouth and giving it a hard suck before he released it with a pop. He absently rolled the wet, pointed flesh between his fingers before he attached the jeweled clamp. He watched her face as he slowly increased the tightness. As soon as she started to pull away from his touch, he stopped, let her get used to it, and when she relaxed, he tightened it just a hair more.

"Ow, ow, ow!"

"Relax. It will go numb soon enough." Leland gave the second nipple the same treatment. When she flinched just as he started to tighten the clamp, he chided. "Nice try, princess, but I know it can be tighter than that."

As soon as the clamps were the way he wanted them, he grabbed her by the hips and set her on the blanket covered workbench that ran along the wall behind her. "Ow. Too hard." She tried to wiggle off the bench, but a slap to the thigh was enough to still her. He pushed her shoulders back until they hit the wall behind her and pulled her hips to the edge of the bench.

"Part of our fun is seeing you two wiggle on your sore asses," the forgotten Kevin said from the other end of the bench where he had Liv laid out on top of the bench with her knees spread open and waiting for his cock, which he had fisted in his hand.

"Holy sh—" Autumn quickly turned away from the scene as a blush spread across her face.

"It is only a cock, princess. Every man has one."

"I know, but he's my boss."

"And I am sure this will only be the first time of many you see him feed his wife his cock." She looked down the length of the bench again. The chief was eagerly pounding into his wife, his fingers working her clit as her breasts bounced with each thrust. A blissful expression graced both of their faces. She turned back to Leland. "Everyone is getting together next weekend, princess. When we get together, it is usually anything but normal. I needed to know how you would react to seeing other nude people and having other people watch us."

"No one will touch you, right?"

He smiled. "No, you are the only one who will touch me, and I will be the only one who will touch you." He slipped two of his fingers inside her eager slit. "You're soaked. Do you like watching or being watched?"

She moaned as he curled his fingers toward the place inside that always did beautiful things to her. Her labored breathing made it difficult to get her answer out. "I guess it *is* kind of hot."

"Good girl." He bent and eagerly took her clit into his mouth.

The added sensation of his suction and rapid tongue movements was enough to send her over the edge. While she was still panting, he slowed his assault on her clit and removed his digits from her heat.

"Your turn?" she questioned, eager to continue what she had tried to start this morning and show him the talents of her mouth.

"Nope, I need at least another hour, but after that..." a dark expression crossed his face "...you are mine."

Chapter 10

Autumn screamed when she was grabbed from behind and dragged into the locker room. "I suggest you be quiet, sub. Unless you want everyone in the firehouse to come looking?"

She relaxed into Leland's arms then let her sass fly. "I don't know, Sir. You were the one who showed me that being watched could be an amazing thing."

He groaned deep in his chest. "I've created a monster."

"Oh, but I am such a fun monster."

"No fun tonight, princess. We have to be on our toes."

Her heart fell, and she turned in the circle of his arms so she could see his face. "Mason got another letter, didn't he?"

"Yes. We will likely have a fire tonight, so I want you to try to get as much sleep as you can. We are all going to need to be at our best."

"Do they have any leads?"

"I don't know, but there's more. Sierra has been put on notice. If there is a fire tonight, she will be reporting live from the scene."

Autumn swallowed hard. "I don't like the thought of her

being there. She isn't like you and me; she doesn't see this stuff regularly."

"I know. I don't like it, either, but she already agreed to do this, and as much as I tried to talk her out of it, she refuses to see reason. Having you there is bad enough. You are only one person, and I can hardly manage to keep an eye on you. I can't watch both of you at the same time."

"PD asked her to do this, so they are going to protect her, right? They are going to have an officer on her, right?"

"Yes." Leland chortled. "In fact, when I went up to the police department to make sure of it, I was told I was already too late in my demands. It turns out both Mason and the chief had beat me to it."

Autumn's smile disappeared. "Not Zander."

"Zander? He doesn't know anything about this."

"Ambulance 23, we have a report of a man down," a disembodied voice called over the loud speaker after the tone sounded.

"Go to work, princess. We'll talk more after your call."

"SOMEONE IS MESSING WITH US."

Autumn glanced at her partner as they strolled into the great room. "Eighteen calls in the past thirteen hours and only two of them turned up real patients. Yeah, someone is messing with us." They collapsed in the first chairs they came across. Autumn laid her head on top of the table. "I need sleep and food, but I am too tired to do the latter or move to the bunks, so I will just sleep here."

"No, you won't, princess."

"I seriously think I hate that nickname. I am anything but a princess."

"You love it when I call you that, and you know it. Now, guys, let's make these girls some food."

"Preferably something we can take with us. The ways the calls are going right now, we will probably be leaving again at any minute," Gwen grumbled from across the table.

"Okay, Gwen, sandwiches, it is," Jensen agreed as he draped a blanket over each of the women before moving to the kitchen.

Autumn woke to the sound of a plate being set next to her head and watched through half-lidded eyes as Jensen picked up Gwen and headed toward the bunks.

"Princess, I am going to put this in a bag. If you have another call, you can eat enroute. Right now, I think you need sleep more than food." With ease, he lifted her into his arms and moved to the couch, where he already had a blanket and pillow waiting.

"I can walk to the bunks, Lee."

"No, I need to hold you, and since we can't go into each other's bunks, the couch will have to do." He lay down, positioning her on top of him, and pulled the blanket over them both. She was asleep in his arms before he had them settled.

"HILL CITY AMBULANCE," Autumn shouted. She had gotten about an hour and a half of sleep. Not nearly enough, but she could at least hold her eyes open as she pounded on the door of the completely dark house, so that was a plus.

If the newspapers scattered at her feet were anything to go by, the owners had been away for a while. "Dispatch, can we get a PD unit to our current location? We can't get into the residence, and no one is answering the door."

"Ten-four."

"Back door is locked as well," Gwen said as she rounded the corner of the house a few seconds later.

"I called for a PD unit," Autumn shared as she hefted the jump bag into the back of the rig before she climbed into the passenger seat to do her paperwork while they waited.

"I swear to God if I have to file one more report that says no patient found, I am going to flip my shit," Gwen complained as she took her seat behind the wheel.

"I know. If I get my hands on the stupid kid who... Did you see that?"

Gwen hit the button to lock the doors. "What? What did you see?"

"I don't know. I thought I saw someone walk out of the alley behind that house." She pointed in front of them as she squinted and tried to find the figure she was sure she had seen.

"Someone coming out of an alley at three in the morning is never a good thing."

Autumn turned back to the computer. "I must have imagined it. It was there one second and gone the next; people don't just disappear."

The sound of the door locks engaging again rang through the rig. "Better safe than sorry. Speaking of safe, how is everything 'safe, sane, and consensual' going between you and the hottie?"

"That was *the* worst lead-in ever."

"Hey, it got the conversation started, didn't it?"

"Yeah, but—"

"Fire!"

Autumn finally looked up from the laptop, her eyes drawn to the red and amber flames dancing in the windows of the house down the block. Shoving the computer back, Autumn jumped from the rig. "Ambulance 23 to dispatch."

"Go ahead, 23."

"We have a fire at the corner of Sherman and 10th! Flames are coming out the second-floor windows!"

"Type of building?"

"Residence." She paused to listen to the sounds around her, her heart dropping to her toes. "I can hear people screaming from inside."

"Fire truck is enroute, 23, four minutes out. Your PD unit is still three minutes out."

One glimpse Gwen's way told Autumn all she needed to know. "Let's go." The last thing they were going to do was stand around the rig listening to the screams.

"Help! Somebody help! Please!"

The frantic voice had both women running. "She has to be at a window! I'll search this side." Autumn sprinted to the side of the house, frantically checking windows for any signs of life as the smoke grew thicker.

"Over here!"

"I don't know if I will be able to catch him!" Gwen yelled at the desperate woman sitting on the ledge of the second-story window as Autumn joined her.

"We are trapped up here! I can't jump down with him in my arms! You have to help! You said you would help!"

"Ma'am, I don't think I can catch him. Two years old or not, I don't—"

"Okay, I'll do it," Autumn interrupted.

"But it's—"

"She has a two-year-old up there, Gwen. Damn right, I'm going to catch him." She turned from her partner. "Okay, ma'am, I'm ready."

"It's cold out there, so you are going to have to get him some-place warm as soon as possible."

"I know, ma'am. The rig is running."

"Autumn, it—"

"Either help me catch him or stop distracting me." Gwen threw her arms in the air and took a sizeable step back. "Okay, on the count of three, toss him down to me. I promise I will catch him. One, two, three!"

Autumn regretted the words as soon as she spoke. Not only did the woman lose her balance and fall out of the window, but it was not a two-year-old child she tossed down, but a snake!

With a scream, she jumped back and let the reptile fall to the ground.

"You said you would catch him! You promised," the panic-stricken woman yelled, paying no mind at all to the obvious deformity of her arm. "Catch him! Catch him before he gets away!"

Autumn shivered as she watched the five-foot snake slither past her before it squeezed under the fence and disappeared. She turned to her partner.

"Don't glare at me like that," Gwen chided. "I tried to warn you. Maybe next time you will listen."

"DID you finally get sick of fighting with the snake lady?"

Autumn looked at the chief. "When she started spitting and throwing dirt at us, we called another rig."

"Good idea." His laughter forced her eyes to roll. "I saw that, sub."

"Are you going to tattle?"

"Nope. It will be more fun watching him try to break you of that nasty habit if I am not the reason you are getting your ass paddled."

"I am going to paddle her ass!" a pissed-off firefighter roared as he stormed around the corner of the house.

Autumn instinctively covered her butt. "Don't worry, girl, he isn't talking about you." Chief gave her shoulder a squeeze then jogged over to cut off the angered man and pull him behind a fire truck a few feet away. "Settle down."

"What is she doing here? She doesn't work on this kind of story." He gestured toward the front of the house.

The man pushed the face shield on his helmet back, revealing his face. Zander. Autumn smiled. She was right; he still loved her.

"She's working this story," the chief calmly answered.

"There is a maniac setting buildings on fire, and they send her? Why?"

"That is none of your concern."

Zander reared back as if he'd been smacked. "None of my concern? I'm her—"

"You're her nothing," Autumn interrupted as she stormed up to the men. "You're. Her. Nothing."

"Autumn," Kevin warned from behind her.

"No, Chief, he needs to hear this, and you pussyfooting around the truth is only going to make matters worse." Autumn saw a brief look of shock on the man's face as she turned back to Zander. "You are nothing to her but an *ex*." The last word had venom dripping from it. "And you have no one but yourself to blame for that. *You* made that choice."

"No, she did. I gave her a choice."

"You gave her *no* choice! You made her choose! You gave her the ultimatum. You told her it was them or you. She thinks of them as family, and you tried to take that away from her."

Zander sputtered for a few seconds before he realized the truth of her words. "Fuck!" Autumn shot an air of disdain in his direction then strutted away, happy with her small victory.

"Leave it to a pissed off sub to tell you exactly how stupid you were." She smiled at Kevin's words.

Gwen smirked when she climbed into the rig. "Finally get to tell Zander how much of a dumbass he is?"

"Oh, yeah."

Chapter 11

A tap on the window caused both Gwen and Autumn to jump.

Hand to her chest, Autumn turned to see a man standing outside her door. Rolling her window down just a crack, she addressed the man, "Can I help you, sir?"

"There is some graffiti on your ambulance, miss."

"What!" She jumped from the rig. Sure enough, a canvas of black spray paint with red lettering decorated the side of the white and blue vehicle. "Shit!"

"Chief, we are going to need you and a couple of Hill City's finest over at the ambulance. We have an issue."

"Ten-four, Gwen."

'Flames engulf your fragile heart.'

"He has left a poem at every fire he has started," an officer in an ill-fitting suit said as he, the chief, and Jensen joined the women.

"I thought the only calling card was the letters Mason got before he set the fires?" The glower Kevin directed at the officer should have killed him on the spot. "You said you were telling us everything."

"We did tell you everything you needed to know."

Kevin took a threatening step forward. "This could be a direct threat to my men! We have a right to know about this!"

"You have no right to know about any of our investigation! Your job is to put out the fire; that is it. The investigation is my job."

"Not for much longer if I can help it." Kevin pulled his phone from his pocket and took a couple of steps away from the rest of them.

"So, ladies, want to tell me how you let this happen to your rig?"

"How we let this happen? You're kidding, right?" Autumn took a step toward the man, Gwen right beside her. "We have jobs like everyone else here does."

"You mean catching snakes?"

"I thought it was a child!" Autumn took another step in the direction of the infuriating man with every intention of socking him in his pasty, round face. An arm wrapped around her middle and lifted her off the ground. "Put me down. I'm going to—"

Before she could finish her threat, a hand had clamped over her mouth and she felt warm breath against her ear. "Quiet, princess. We have his behavior on tape, but if you finish that threat, you will be in jail. You can lick my hand all you want, sub, but if you bite me, I will drag you into the back of the ambulance and paddle your ass." She let her lips cover her teeth once more. He knew her too well. "Good choice. Now, I am going to take my hand off your mouth. The only things I want to hear from your mouth are direct answers to his questions. Understood?"

Her "yes, Sir" was hindered by his hand, but he must have understood because he removed his hand. While wiping it on his bunker pants, he nodded at the officer. "What was your question, officer?"

"Actually, I am a detective, Detective Starling, and I advise that you address me correctly."

Anger bubbled in Autumn's gut. She briefly glanced back at her partner for support, but the woman didn't look like she was having any easier time containing her rage. She was on her own. "Can you repeat your question, *detective*?"

"How did you let this happen?"

"We didn't let anything happen."

"The reporter wants to interview you," another officer said as he joined them. "I will finish with these guys for you." As soon as the Detective Starling was out of earshot, the young officer talked. "Sorry about him. I promise some of us use the manners our mothers drilled into us. Let's try this again. I'm Officer Thomas. Can you tell me when was the last time you saw the ambulance without the new paint job?"

"It was clean when we arrived on the scene of our original call, so about 0310, but I don't know the exact time without looking at the logged time."

He nodded toward the rig. Autumn didn't give him the chance to change his mind and was pulling up the necessary information as she half listened to the questions he was now directing at Gwen.

"I didn't see anything unusual." Gwen paused for a second. "But Autumn thought she saw someone come out of the alley behind the house probably five minutes before we called it in."

She turned from the computer as realization dawned. "I saw the arsonist, didn't I?"

"It is possible."

"Why does she seem so excited about that possibility?" Leland looked like he was never going to let her go on a call without him again.

"Do you know what time that was?"

"I can tell you exactly the time. I had just started the paper-work; the program notes every time it's opened." She hit a few more keys. "We arrived on scene at 0308, and I saw the person come out of the alley at 0323."

The officer flipped back a few pages in his notes. "You called in the fire six minutes after you saw the person. Any chance he stepped under a street lamp, and you have a description to give me? Yeah, I didn't think so."

Chapter 12

She looked ridiculous. Utterly and completely ridiculous.

"Wow."

"That's it? That is all you have to say? Liv, I look absurd!" Autumn collapsed into a chair.

"First, don't let any of the tops hear you say that. When we all get together, no sub is safe. They won't discipline you, but they will rat you out in a heartbeat, and speaking badly of yourself will be the fastest way to get any one of them to do just that. Second, my 'wow' was not intended to be negative. You look stunning, and he didn't make you wear heels?"

She peered down her body, past the simple thigh-length black dress to her lime green high tops. "He didn't have much of a choice. I can't walk in those deathtraps." Her friend laughed. "No, really. I practiced all day yesterday, and I nearly broke my neck countless times."

"It's true. The only thing forcing her to wear those shoes would have accomplished was a night spent in the emergency room," Leland shared as he sauntered into the room with Kevin right behind him.

"Touch your toes." Liv instantly turned and bent at her waist; her ass facing her husband.

"You, too, sub," Leland demanded as his gaze landed on Autumn. She sputtered for a few seconds before she took her place next to Liv and did as she was ordered. "Both of you look lovely tonight. As usual." He knelt behind her and gave her calves a squeeze before he ran his hands up her legs to the hem of her dress. "I wanted to make sure you did as you were told and skipped the panties, princess."

The end of her skirt brushed against the swell of her ass as he slowly pulled the back of it up, bunching it at her waist to expose her naked behind. She was not sure if the quiver that ran through her was a result of the cold air meeting her heated pussy or his finger running over her dark pucker. It didn't matter; all that mattered at that moment was the groan of pleasure that rumbled from Leland's chest and his next words.

"Good girl, princess." He patted her bare, lower lips with the flat of his hand before he pulled her dress back in place and helped her to stand. He kissed her hard on the mouth, chuckling when she buried her fingers in his hair. "We have to go play good host, baby. We do not have time for the kiss to go any deeper." He pried her fingers from his hair and smiled at her pout. "We will play later, promise, but right now, Sierra is waiting for you in the kitchen."

She was attacked as soon as she stepped into the kitchen. "Where have you been? I have not seen you in weeks! Lee is stealing you away from me!"

She wrapped her arms around Sierra, giving her a tight squeeze. "I just saw you at the last fire, only two days ago."

"That was work. Work doesn't count."

"Okay, I saw you last weekend at breakfast."

Sierra stepped out of the hug so she could see her friend's face. "See what I mean? A whole week. He is taking up all your time. You have no idea what is going on in my life."

She laughed as she took a cup out of the cupboard and filled it with water. "You are *so* dramatic. Fill me in on what is happening in your life."

"Zander apologized."

Autumn coughed, spitting water everywhere. "He said he was sorry? Like sincerely?" Her conversation with him at the fire came to mind as she dabbed her friend's face dry with a hand towel.

"Seemed sincere to me."

She took Sierra's face in her hands. "Tell me you did not take him back just because he said sorry."

"Are you nuts?"

"Good." The sigh of relief was out before she could stop it.

"I love him. He is my Daddy and always will be, but I do not wish to put myself through that heartache again. Taking responsibility for the hurt he caused me was a huge step, but that was just the first step. He has like a trillion more to go, and they are all uphill. Besides, I'm kind of busy being with someone else."

Autumn laughed, happy to see that her friend had stood up for herself and refused to let the man off the hook so easily. "I am proud of you, Sierra, but you have to tell me who this someone else is."

"So you can run to my brother? Absolutely not."

"I'm proud of her, too." The girls turned toward the back door.

"Zander, a pleasure to see you again." If Sierra thought she was fooling anyone with her nonchalant attitude, she was sorely mistaken.

The man chuckled. "I didn't mean to interrupt. I was just coming in to refill my glass."

"Nope, nothing to interrupt here. If you will excuse me, I have to go find... someone." With that, Sierra flounced out of the kitchen with her head held high.

"I am *so* damn proud of her. Don't look so surprised." He

smiled as he watched Sierra through the patio doors. "She has grown so much since I fucked everything up. She is stronger and more sure of herself while somehow maintaining that innocent little quality about her."

"You love her." It wasn't a question. Autumn could hear it in his words and see it in the way he stared at her.

"I never stopped loving her." He turned to Autumn. "I saw Mason and Tabby as competition, and by letting my jealousy get the best of me, I took it out on her. I didn't see them for what they were until you pointed it out."

"Your shortsightedness hurt her."

"I know. Mason and Leland both made sure that I knew precisely how much I had hurt her."

"I hope they got some good hits in when they kicked your ass."

He rubbed his jaw as if it was still tender. "Your Dom has quite the right hook."

"Yeah, his left arm has some significant power behind it, too, that is for sure." Without thinking, she reached back to rub her bottom. "So what are you going to do to fix your colossal mistake?"

His smile showed off his white teeth. "I am going to let her go."

"She loves you."

"I know, but if my stepping away has gotten her to grow this much, I can't hinder that. She deserved to grow and evolve, and this mystery man has done just that, so I step away and let him take the lead."

"She is still going to make you suffer." Autumn left the laughing man in the kitchen.

"Is Zander going to tell me that you were rude to him, princess?"

"I just stepped out onto the deck, Sir, so how could I have possibly misbehaved already?"

"Can you blame me for my worrying, sub? The last time you talked to Zander, you told him in no uncertain terms exactly how much of an idiot he had been."

"I told him the truth, which he needed to hear. Just like you did, Sir. The only difference is I didn't use my fists to relay the message."

Leland threw his head back and laughed. "Told you about that, did he?"

"Yes, Sir. We compared notes on the power of your swing."

AUTUMN LAUGHED SO HARD, she snorted. "You're kidding?"

"Honest to God!" Liv raised her hands to the heavens and laughter exploded from the circle of women once more.

"How does that happen?" Sierra asked as she wiped the tears from the corner of her eyes.

Liv tried desperately to catch her breath. "I don't know. One minute, I was bent over the kitchen counter getting my ass spanked, and the next, I heard a groan of pain from Kevin. When I turned around to see what had happened, he was bent over in agony."

"Olivia, are you sharing the forbidden story?" Kevin joined the group with a smirk playing on his lips, his presence fueling the women's laughter.

"But, Sir, it's a funny story."

He rolled his eyes then turned from his wife to the rest of the submissives who were trying so desperately to keep their giggle to themselves. "Go on, ask."

Autumn looked around the circle. Everyone was trying to determine if this was a trap, and if it was, would the laugh be worth the possible consequence? With a deep breath, she threw caution to the wind as respectfully as possible, of course, and asked what everyone was itching to know. "How does that happen, Sir?"

"You mean how did I manage, while punishing my sub, to miss her ass and, instead, hit myself in the groin?"

Autumn bit her cheek to fight off the smile threatening to surface. "Yes, Sir. That is what we would like to know."

"When you figure it out, let me know, because I have absolutely no idea how in the hell I managed to rack myself."

Laughter rolled through the gathering, and she watched as Kevin turned to his wife with an evil twinkle in his dark eyes. When she opened her mouth to warn her friend, a heavy hand landed on her shoulder. "Let them be, princess. He warned her what the telling of that story would cost her. She, alone, decided it was worth the price."

"Sub." The one word was enough to get the attention of everyone in the small group, but Kevin only had eyes for his wife, who was now red-faced and looking at the ground, a smile playing on the corner of her lips.

"Yes, Sir?"

"Do you remember our agreement?"

"Of course, I do, Sir."

Without a word, Kevin gestured to the waist-high deck railing. Chewing her lip, Olivia walked to the designated area and bent over the rail. When he turned to the group once more, all eyes were on him. "Olivia and I had an agreement. She could tell people of my unfortunate episode, but for each person she told, they or their perspective Dom gets to take three swings at her beautiful ass."

"Three! We agreed on one for each person I told!"

"No, you *demanded* one. I wanted there to be a chance that my embarrassing story would be kept between the two of us, so we *agreed* on three. You and I both know that one swat from everyone would not be a deterrent for you at all. I can see in your eyes that you remember. If I had been thinking, I would have made the number of strikes higher, but we agreed to three, and three it shall be. Now, turn back around and bend over the rail, sub."

As soon as Olivia was where he wanted her, he walked up behind her and lifted her skirt, exposing her creamy nates. "So, who heard the story of my misfortune from the lips of my girl, here?"

Autumn watched as an alarming number of people stepped forward. The Doms were quick to rat out the unfortunate submissive, but on the other hand, hesitation showed on the faces of most every sub.

"Princess?"

"Look at how many people she told, and they all get to take a swing at her?"

"Yes, and you were one of them."

"You want me to *spank* her? There are so many others. I'm sure my lack of participation will go unnoticed, Sir."

"If you are uncomfortable with this, princess, no one will force you to take part. I will give her the owed smacks on your behalf."

"Like hell!" Autumn's hand clamped over her mouth as soon as the bitter, snarled words escaped her mouth and the dark, unhappy expression crossed his face. "I'm so sorry, Sir!" The hand that shot out to tangle in her hair told her just how unpleased he was.

"I don't know what gave you the impression that your attitude would be received well, but don't worry, princess, I will make sure your mouth doesn't get the better of you again." The tug on her hair forced her to her knees on the smooth, unrelenting wood of the deck in front of him, putting her face and mouth exactly where he wanted it. All in the middle of the small group of friends. "Spread your knees. Further. Good girl." The touch of the cool breeze brushing against her bare pussy forced a whimper to escape from her throat. "You decide to run your mouth in front of our guests, then I will decide to put your mouth to good use in front of guests."

"Sir," she pleaded as he worked the buttons of his fly with his free hand, never releasing her hair from his tight hold.

"Don't speak," he growled as his partially erect member sprang free of the confines of his jeans. "Unless you are saying your safe word, you have lost your privilege to speak for the rest of the night. Now, naughty pet, open your mouth and mind your teeth." The pleading expression she shot his way did her no good, and when he arched his brow, she instantly opened her mouth and allowed him to feed her his cock. His warm skin tasted salty against her tongue. "You are to suck me dry and swallow every last drop."

As she went to work, sucking and swirling her tongue, the conversation picked up where it left off as if seeing a woman on her knees pleasuring a man was nothing. With her head bobbing, Autumn watched the people around her. They all seemed to be ignoring her, but she could not shake the notion that everyone was watching her.

A sharp tug of her hair forced her to gasp around his cock before it fell from her mouth. "Your concentration should be on me and me alone. Does my cock bore you?"

"No, Sir. I-I just…"

He tucked himself back into his pants before he took a knee in front of her and spoke in a soothing tone. "You are exaggerating the number of people here, princess, and you are letting them overwhelm you." When she tried to look down, he stopped her by grasping her chin. "At most, there are fifteen people here, including us. You know and trust every one of them. Hell, you trust most of them with your life on a regular basis during any one of our calls. So please, tell me what is keeping you from submitting to me."

"I." She took a deep breath. "When I went to the clubs, the people watching me were faceless strangers, but these are my friends and colleagues. What if they use my submission against me?"

"Look at them and point out one person here who you think will judge you for your submission?" He gave her a few minutes to appraise the group of their friends. When her eyes returned to him, he smiled. "Couldn't come up with anyone, could you?"

A smile graced her lips. "No, Sir. I trust them. Thank you for giving me the time to remember that."

"You're welcome, princess. Now…" he stood "…finish what you started."

She removed his cock from his pants then grabbed his thighs and eagerly took his dick into her mouth. This time, she was able to give the rapidly growing appendage the attention she knew he sought as the voices and people of the party melted away. She swirled her tongue around the head before she glided the flat of her tongue along the bulging vein on the underside of the shaft.

He only allowed her control for a few minutes before fisting her hair and holding her in the position he wanted. "Do you like teasing me to the point of madness?" He didn't give her the opportunity to answer before he started driving into her mouth. With each thrust, he went deeper until he butted against the back of her throat, causing her to gag. "Breathe when I pull back, princess. I know you can do this, but if you panic, tap my thigh, and I will stop."

Autumn closed her eyes and focused on his back and forth movements, thankful he had taken over and set the pace. The added tug on her hair combined with the surrender of the last bit of control she had allowed her to relax and focus on what he asked of her. She hollowed her cheeks and sucked harder. The groan of pleasure that vibrated from his chest forced her core to clench, drawing her attention to the slickness that had gathered between her spread thighs.

His leg muscles bunched under her hands, indicating he was

close, so she moaned around his shaft. The vibrations did as she hoped, and she felt the first burst of cum explode in her mouth.

"Swallow it!" His demand was strangled.

When he finally relaxed under her hands, he pulled free of her mouth and tucked his cock back into his pants. With a smile on his face, he crouched in front of her and wiped at the corner of her mouth with his thumb. "Open up, princess. You missed some."

Chapter 13

Who knew a woman—no, your woman—lapping a dribble of cum from your thumb could make your cock stir so enthusiastically so soon after coming?

He pulled his thumb from her mouth with a pop and stood in front of her. "You are going to kneel here for a few minutes. Don't look at me with that pout. You are crazy if you think I am going to reward you with an orgasm of you own, princess. The blowjob was supposed to be a punishment or at least make you uncomfortable while you are punished." He reached under her skirt and ran his fingers along her slit. The second he felt her warm cream against his fingers, a groan rumbled from his chest, and a smile split his face. He adjusted her skirt to expose her pussy, allowing the breeze of the night to caress her skin without interference. "You will remain here, feeling the breeze on your hot, unclothed pussy while you think about why you are kneeling here, knees spread with my seed still coating your lips."

"Yes, Sir." He kissed her forehead then strode over to stand beside Kevin, making sure to stay within her line of sight.

"I was starting to think I was never going to see this day."

"What day?"

"The day Leland Boisy doesn't want to display his sub's assets for all to see. Tell me, does she know that even though you raised her skirt, no one can see a thing because of the way you draped the fabric across her legs?"

A smirk played at the corners of his lips. "If I did it correctly, no." He sobered, looking his best friend in the eye. "She is more than just my submissive, Kev. She is my girl, my lover, my princess. She is mine."

"Shit, you're planning a forever with her."

Leland knew it was not a question, but when he turned to Autumn again, the need to answer struck him hard in the chest. "Yeah, she's my forever."

The men stood there in silence for a long time, both staring at the women they loved, before Kevin spoke. "I suspect the arsonist intentionally set the last fire for Gwen and Autumn to find."

His heart constricted in his chest. "The marshal got another letter."

"Yeah. More than likely, we will have another fire next shift. The girls have the day off."

He turned to Kevin sharply as mixed feelings of appreciation and apprehension filled his chest. "If you're forcing them to take a day off, that means you are worried about them."

"It wasn't my call; the firebug mentioned both Autumn and Gwen in the letter. The higher-ups are giving them the day off with pay."

"What did it say?" When he didn't answer fast enough, Leland turned to his friend and got dangerously quieter. "What did it say?"

"Our speculations were right. Autumn saw him step out of the alley, and while she was unable to make out his face, the light in the cab allowed him to see them. He is no longer just obsessed with your sister, Lee. He has taken an interest in Gwen and Autumn as well."

Dread settled into his gut. "Fuck! It was bad enough with Sierra, but I can't keep an eye on both of them." He started to pace in the small area. "I can probably talk her into taking one shift off, but no way will she go for more than that, and that still leaves Sierra in the thick of things."

"Someone else is going to cover the next fire. The hope is that in denying him the presence of the requested women, he will become agitated and reveal himself to us. It's only one shift. She can handle missing one day of work. Then we hope like hell the next fire is the one he messes up on and, in turn, becomes his last."

Leland shook his head in agreement as the need to hold and protect forced his feet to move. He plucked her off the ground so suddenly that a tiny squeal escaped. "Sorry, princess. It's just me." With her safely wrapped in his arms, he collapsed into a chair and just held her, letting the weight of her cuddled into his chest slowly dissipate the nauseating fear inside him.

Chapter 14

The vibrating in her pocket woke Autumn with a start. She was face down on her bed, feet hanging off, her tennis shoes still on her feet. It was her required day off, and Liv had done everything she could to get her mind off work. Shopping, pedicures, manicures, more shopping, lunch at a way too expensive restaurant, and more shopping. Thank God this was a paid day off because her checking account had taken a huge hit.

"Hello?" she questioned as she rolled onto her back and wedged the phone between her shoulder and ear.

"Where are you?" Leland growled from the other end of the phone line.

"I just got home about..." She glanced over at the clock. Any remaining sleepiness was forced from her head by the slight tone of worry in his voice. "About thirty minutes ago."

"Oh, thank God."

"Why? What's wrong? It's too early for the arsonist to have started the fire already!"

"No, no, he hasn't set anything ablaze yet. There was a crash on the interstate; they sent some of the guys. Since you hadn't

108

called to tell me you were home yet, I got worried." His tone held the slightest bit of reproach.

"I'm sorry, Sir. I was so tired from chasing every sale Liv could find that I flopped down on my bed when I got home and passed out. I didn't mean to scare you."

"It's okay, princess. You didn't break any rules, just our routine. I only had a little heart attack," he teased. "You are just never allowed to take a day off without me again."

"This one was forced on me, remember? And if I did that, you would never get a sexy surprise ever again, Sir."

A mixture of a moan and growl rumbled over the line, before Autumn heard some of the guys talking in the background. "As much as I hate to cut this conversation short just as it is getting to the good part, I have to go eat before one of my *brothers* steals my food right off my plate."

"I can just feel the brotherly love from here." Autumn laughed.

"That is how the brotherhood works. They will risk their life to protect me, but I am never safe from their antics, which means my food is fair game to whatever they decide, be that eating it or sabotaging it. Okay, I have to go. Have fun with Sierra tonight. I will pick you up from there when my shift is over in the morning. Zander! Step away from the sandwich, and no one gets hurt," Leland demanded right before the line went dead.

"I HAD to drive three hours to the campsite to give Leland clothes so he didn't have to run around naked for the rest of the weekend, not that he had any real issue with it. The rest of the guys were the ones bitching because their 'awesome' prank had backfired, and Lee was happily strutting around in all his naked glory." Sierra raised her hand in the air in an effort to show how honest she was being.

Autumn wiped a tear from her eye as she tried to catch her breath. "Why would they steal all his clothes? And more importantly, why would they keep going on this trip if they knew it would be full of practical jokes?"

"I asked the same thing while I was there. Sitting around the campfire with about two dozen grown men, half of which unknowingly had a penis or some crude saying written on their face in marker. They told me their shift had been doing it for years, and none of them planned to stop anytime soon."

"Let me guess, it is part of being brothers and it 'strengthens the bond?'"

"Exactly what they said. I am so glad women don't show their love by stealing clothes and drawing on each other's faces."

"Well, we do, but we call it doing our makeup and borrowing clothes." Autumn laughed at her own joke.

"You work that shift. Have you ever been invited?"

"Of course, I have, but I always felt being stuck in the woods with a bunch of men I have seen way too much of already would be super weird, and after that story and the stories I have heard over the years, it seems I was right."

Sierra's phone started to ring. Taking a few seconds to compose herself, she wiped the tears from her face and cleared her throat before looking at her lap and answering her phone in a solemn manner. "Hello?"

It didn't take many words from the person on the other line for Sierra to look up quickly and lock eyes with Autumn. Something was wrong.

"Yes, sir. I will meet the cameraman there." Pause. "No, I have someone to drive me. I will do my camera makeup enroute." Sierra held the phone to her ear as she took off running toward her bedroom. When she emerged five minutes later, she was in a pair of black slacks, a lightweight maroon sweater, a pair of nude colored flats, and her makeup bag was in hand. "Let's go. You're driving."

Autumn ran to the door. She knew from past reporter emergencies with Sierra that they had to move quickly. "What's going on?" Autumn questioned as she backed the car out of the driveway.

"We are going to the north part of town. There is a house on fire."

Autumn stopped in the middle of the road. "We were told to stay away from this fire."

"I know, but when my boss calls and tells me to move, I move."

"Sierra, I—"

"You can either drive me, or I can go by myself. Either way, I am going to report on this fire. My boss was the reporting party, so we have a leg up on the other news stations, and from what my boss says, the fire is moving quickly. So, either drive the car, or get out so I can."

She started driving. "There is no way in hell I am letting you do this alone."

"You know there is a good chance you will get into trouble for going to the scene, right?"

"Yeah, by both my boss and your brother." Uneasiness settled in the pit of Autumn's stomach, and it had nothing to do with the possible consequences and everything to do with gut instinct.

Chapter 15

When the tone sounded through the station, it forced Leland from his bunk and sent him racing down the hall to the fire poles. As soon as he landed on the first floor, he took off running to his gear outside the ladder truck. He shoved his feet into his boots and pulled up his bunker pants as a disembodied voice announced the details of the fire.

"We have a report of a house fire on the corner of Frank and 3rd. Reporting party says he can hear screaming and crying from inside the building. He also states he saw a person in the second-story window. Report of a house fire at Frank and 3rd. Unknown number of people inside."

The knowledge that people were trapped in the house got Leland and his brothers moving that much faster. "Let's roll, boys," Zander shouted as he climbed behind the wheel of the ladder truck, the engine roaring to life a few seconds later.

Leland pulled himself up into the truck and looked at each of his brothers. They all nodded, silently letting each other know they were ready to put their lives on the line to save the lives of any unknown individuals.

Seated across from him, Jensen did what he did before every

fire. As usual, every man in the truck joined him in reciting the "Fireman's Prayer."

As the prayer ended, they pulled to a stop in front of a two-story home, and the men in the truck fell silent. They all took a second to take in the sight in front of them before they jumped into action.

As soon as Leland's booted feet landed on the pavement, a heavy SCBA unit was shoved up his arms and onto his back before the mask was placed in his hands.

"Tanks on!" Leland glanced over his shoulder just in time to see Zander turn to help Jensen with his pack.

With all the safety checks finished and his mask sealed around his face, Leland put his helmet on his head and climbed to the top of the ladder truck then followed Jensen up to the second-story window.

WATCHING Leland climb into a burning building stole the breath from Autumn's lungs. She was usually so busy getting ready for possible patients that she had never actually watched him disappear into the thick, black smoke before that night.

Shaking herself, Autumn grabbed a pair of gloves from the glove compartment as she abandoned her car. She easily got through the crowd of gathered people, and when she got to the officers holding the crowd at bay, all she had to do was tell them she was a paramedic and show them her gloved hands and everyone let her by. Knowing how easy it was to get past the police tape had a lump forming in her gut.

Was that how the arsonist had gotten close enough to the scene to vandalize the rig? Was he impersonating a crewmember?

"I was about to call you in for additional help." Kevin sounded relieved when he finally noticed her. He handed her a radio and headed closer to the house, tossing his next words over his shoulder. "The radio is set to fire frequency. When they say they are bringing someone out, I want you all to be ready. The second rig is already here; you and Gwen have yours!"

It took all Autumn had to drag her eyes away from the smoke rolling out of the house in front of her. "How many do they think are in there?"

"A family of four lives here, so as far as we know, four people are trapped inside."

As soon as she finished talking, a frantic man burst through the police barricades. "Catch him!" a police officer yelled as the man headed for the front door, completely disregarding the smoke billowing out of it.

Just as the man was about to step onto the porch, Kevin plowed into him, taking him to the ground. The two rolled in the dirt for a few seconds before the cops were able to pull the troubled man off the chief.

"My family is in there!" the man screamed as he fought against the officers with everything he had. "My family is in there!"

Having enough of the scene playing out before her, Autumn marched up to the man who was now being held by three struggling officers. As soon as she got close enough, she reached out and slapped the screaming man as hard as she could across the face. When he went silent, she started talking. "You are acting like an idiot and keeping these men from being able to help your family. Help us help them and tell us how many people are in the house." When he was slow in answering, Autumn again demanded, "How many people are in the house!"

"Two! Only two. My son was at a friend's house. I just picked him up. He is in the car down the street."

"Then, who is in the house?"

"My wife and our other son! You have to get them! You have to save them!"

Autumn looked at the officers and got a nod of approval

before she continued her questions. "Where in the house would they be? The firefighters need to know where to find them."

"My son would be in his bedroom. It's at the back of the house, on the second floor."

As soon as he finished talking, Kevin spoke into his radio. "Confirmed one male child and a female adult in the house. The child should be on the second floor in the bedroom on the north side of the house. I repeat; the kid is in the north portion of the second floor."

"Ten-four. We don't have much time left with the roof, Chief."

"Where is your wife?" Autumn questioned, frantically trying to get the needed information so she could get her colleagues out of the house.

The desperate man covered his face with his hands. "I don't know! Sometimes she waits to go to sleep until I get home. Other nights, she can't help but fall asleep."

Kevin spoke in a no-nonsense tone. "When she goes to sleep before you get home, does she go to bed, or does she fall asleep someplace else?"

"I-I don't know!"

"One more room to search up here," a disembodied voice announced from the radios surrounding Autumn.

"Sir, I need to know where to find your wife, and I need to know now! The house is starting to collapse, so I can only allow my men to remain in the building for a few more minutes. Do you understand? Very soon, I am going to have to pull my guys out of the house whether I find your wife and kid or not, so I suggest you help us find her by telling us where she usually falls asleep when she is waiting for you!"

Something Kevin said must have broken through to the man because the desired information fell from his lips, "The couch in the family room. She usually falls asleep on the sofa in front of the television."

"What side of the house?" Kevin demanded, panic evident in his voice.

"Northeast corner."

"We have the kid!"

"Okay, Boisy, Clark, get out. Horris, Mote, it is possible that the wife is in the back northeast corner of the house."

"Already searched it, Chief. Didn't find anyone."

"Then clear out," Kevin demanded into his mic.

"No! You can't do that! My wife! My wife is in there!" The man started to fight against the cops once again.

"Sir, where did you park your car? Where is your other child?" Autumn asked the desperate man while she followed him as the cops dragged him away from the house.

"Ma'am, you are going to need to step back," an officer advised as he ran up to the group to aid his fellow officers.

Just as Autumn opened her mouth to argue, her elbow was caught in a rough grasp, and she was physically hauled back to the safety of the street. "Hey! Stop! Let go of me, you jackass!" A growl rumbled from under the mask still attached to the fireman's face as he tore it off and she was pinned in place by the deep brown eyes of her extremely unhappy Dom, and there was no question he was fully in his Dom. "Oh, Lee! Thank God, you are all right!" If she were not physically being held in place by the man, she would have hugged him.

"What the hell are you doing? Do you know how dangerous it is to be that close to a fire, let alone that close to a man who has very possibly lost everything tonight?" Leland demanded when he finally pulled her to a stop between a couple of the trucks.

"The cops were struggling to get information from him, so I helped."

The expression on Leland's face could only be described as complete and utter shock. "We will discuss the ridiculousness of your actions in the morning. Right now, I want you out of here.

You were to be absent from the scene tonight. Go home, princess."

"I can't. I am on duty now. Even if I wasn't, I can't just leave your sister here with no ride home," Autumn replied with far too much sass for a woman who knew she was already in trouble.

"So, not only did you put yourself in danger, but you put my sister in danger, too?"

The rumble of his voice made her shiver a bit, but she wasn't going to back down now. "Your sister is doing her job as well. Her boss called her in, and you know she would have driven herself had I refused to drive."

Leland wiped his soot-covered face with his gloved hand as he sighed. A kiss was roughly placed on her forehead before he walked back to talk to Kevin. She had won round one.

Autumn didn't move from where he left her. The truth was she needed a little time to catch her breath. She knew going up to the disturbed man would get her into trouble, but she just couldn't help it. She saw a man whom she knew would soon regret his choice to withhold the needed information, and she could not stand forcing him to live with that guilt for the rest of his life if she could get him to help.

She watched as her fellow paramedics loaded the young boy into the rig and took off, sirens whirling.

"I thought you were supposed to have the night off?"

Autumn turned to her partner, who was scribbling on the clipboard she clutched in her hands. "When did you get here?"

Gwen tore her eyes from the clipboard and gestured to the second rig parked on the other side of the street. As she opened her mouth to talk, an awful noise came from the house.

The front wall of the brick building creaked and groaned as it started to fall. Autumn opened her mouth to warn Kevin and Leland, who were standing in front of it, but she was too late. She had no choice but to watch everything happen in slow motion.

She saw it on Kevin's face as soon as the decision was made. Instead of running when he saw the wall of bricks coming at him, Kevin sprinted the three steps it took him to get to Leland and shoved him with everything he had.

A high-pitched scream pierced the dark night, pulling Autumn from her frozen stupor. She spared a single glance at the screaming woman, Sierra, who was being held back by a determined Zander. He didn't seem to notice that the thrashing woman was pounding on his chest with everything she had. He simply wrapped her in his arms and rocked her as he pressed his soot-covered face into her hair.

The screaming continued as Autumn took off running toward the smoldering pile of rubble and the flames beyond it. With every step she took, she felt like she took four steps back as her vision tunneled. Nearly everyone who wasn't manning a hose or controlling the crowd rushed to the pile of ruins where Kevin was last seen. Firefighters and cops alike were running right past the unconscious Lee and digging through the crumbled brick to find the chief.

When she finally reached the debris, she went directly to Leland's side. He lay on the edge of the pile, the lower half of his body pinned under a slab of bricks and his head bleeding from the impact of his fall.

Her training kicked in, and as hard as it was to ignore the tightness in her chest, she started barking orders to a couple of the firefighters. "You three, I need this slab lifted off his legs. I need to assess the damage. You two! I need the cot out of the rig, and while you are over there, see if you can get my associates to move their asses!"

"That is the second time tonight you have sworn, princess," Leland croaked as he tried to lift his head.

"Don't move!" The demand was swift, and she immediately had one of the firefighters hold his head in place. "I need to get you into a collar and—"

Leland's laugh and resulting grunt of pain when his body jostled interrupted Autumn's babbling. "That's funny. I always thought I would be the one putting a collar on you."

"How can you be laughing and carrying on like this? This isn't funny, Lee!" She could do nothing to keep the tears from pooling in her eyes as she fitted the c-collar around his neck. "You were just hit by a smoking pile of bricks, and you think now is an appropriate time to laugh?"

"Who is in charge?" he demanded as he was rolled to his side and someone shoved the backboard under him. When they rolled him back to his back, his eyes locked with Autumn's. "I asked you a question, and I expect to be answered, sub."

A blush spread across Autumn's face as the combination of adrenaline and fear had her heart threatening to pound out of her chest. "This is not the time nor the place for this. You are hurt. We need to get you to a hospital." When his arrogant brow didn't descend from its elevated position, she relented, "You are, usually, but you are my patient now, so for right now, I am in charge."

A few of the men chuckled as they loaded him into the rig. Leland just smiled as he spoke. "I won't be your patient for long, princess. You will soon be back over my knee." Autumn climbed into the ambulance and attached the necessary monitors. Gwen climbed in and ordered one of the firemen to get ready to drive as she applied a tourniquet and started an IV. "The tears staining your cheeks are contradicting your smile, princess."

"Leland, I am giving you some meds for the pain. They are going to make you tired."

"A few tears never hurt anyone." Leland smiled when she used his own words against him.

Autumn watched as the drugs took effect, and Leland let his eyes droop closed. She reached forward and grabbed his hand before she closed her own eyes and allowed the tears to flow freely. "I love you, Sir."

Chapter 16

The flags that lined the roads were brought to life by the breeze, their movement the only sound in the quiet cemetery. With tears in her eyes, Autumn looked at the line of firefighters in their navy-blue jackets standing on the other side of the casket. They stood perfectly still, prepared to make the final salute to their fallen brother. Mason was the exception; he stood at the end of the line holding a small hammer, poised above a bronze bell.

Olivia pulled her hand from Autumn's grasp as Jensen knelt in front of her with the folded flag in his arms. "Liv, we are all here to support you in any way we can. All you have to do is call." He paused for a second. "Who am I kidding? You will be so sick of us showing up at your door, but that is what we do for family. Kevin was an amazing man and brother. He will be missed for a long time."

With tears running down her face, Olivia took the flag and clutched it to her chest before she brokenly replied, "Thank you. Even knowing the outcome, the st-stupid man would probably do it all over again, wouldn't he?"

"We all would have done the same thing to save one of our

brothers." With a kiss to her forehead, Jensen stood and joined the rest of the firefighters.

Olivia turned and buried her face in Autumn's shoulder just as the bronze bell was rung, signaling the end of Kevin's call to duty. With each tone of the bell, Olivia jumped in her seat, and her cries got louder.

AT THE SOUND of the final bell, Autumn sat straight up in bed. Her eyes snapped open when Lee wrapped his strong arms around her and pulled her to his chest, the sweat on her face making his coarse chest hair itchy against her cheek.

"It was just a nightmare, baby," he whispered as he crushed her further into his torso, temporarily stealing her breath away.

"But it isn't just a dream." Sobs broke her words into many syllables. "I feel so horrible! I thank God every day that it wasn't you, but then I remember Kevin died and how much Liv lost because he chose to save you instead of himself."

"There is no reason for you to feel guilty. No one chose for him. He, alone, made that choice. He did what any one of us would have done." He gathered a fistful of Autumn's hair and gently pulled her face away from his chest so he could gaze into her eyes.

Autumn scowled at him. He had been telling her that for six weeks now, and the fact that any of the other men would have done the same did little to make her feel any better. No matter what he said to ease her guilt, the rock still sat heavily in the bottom of her stomach, right next to the horrible feeling that he didn't want her any longer. "Of course, there is a reason for me to feel guilty! I'm thanking God for killing another man! I am thanking God for sparing the man I love, who I *thought* loved me in return, while another woman has lost her whole world!"

"Thought?"

The confused expression on the clueless man's face only served to piss her off. "Yes, thought! You have been avoiding your sub for weeks! At first, I thought that maybe you were just waiting until you could put weight on your leg, but the doctor put you in a walking cast weeks ago!"

"Autumn, we have been having sex every couple of nights for the past few weeks."

"I know, *Sir*, I was there, but you haven't done anything else!" Autumn saw the light click on in his head. "Are you getting it now, Dom Dom?"

When she rolled her eyes at him, Leland twisted her dark hair tightly around his fist. The quick, sharp pain forced a gasp from her lips as his left brow rose toward his hairline. "Are you allowed to roll your eyes at me, sub?"

Her built-up hurt and anger prevented her from heeding his warning. "Oh, so you remember that I am the sub to your Dom now, huh?"

"I have never forgotten that you are mine, but it seems you have forgotten who you belong and answer to."

She again rolled her eyes. The resulting growl that echoed from Leland's chest did nothing to break through her sarcasm. "Could have fooled me. You have all but thrown our rules and the resulting consequences out the window. Hell, if I would have talked to you like this before the fire, you would have been slapping my ass before I had finished speaking." Autumn scoffed. "Now, I have rolled my eyes at you two times and called you a dumb Dom, and still you have done nothing! I am blatantly disrespecting you, but here I sit. Sit being the operative word. I cannot handle not knowing what to expect!"

Leland released her hair and forced her to look in to his eyes by putting his hands on either side of her face. "Autumn, I believed I was giving you the time you needed to deal with the loss of a dear friend. I had no idea I was letting you down. Why didn't you tell me what you needed? That I was slacking?"

She tried to turn away, but he held her captive. The little show of tender dominance instantly had tears welling in her eyes. "It's hard to ask for help. Every time I talked myself into requesting what I knew I needed, I would see your cast, and I would have more guilt for needing you when you were already struggling with your own healing. It quickly became a vicious cycle."

Leland sat up in bed and pulled her to straddle his hips. "Autumn, I'm so sorry I didn't see what you needed from me before now. I should have, and for that, I am sorry, but you know we have to communicate with each other. I cannot read your mind, no matter how much easier it would make things. Yes, I know I usually am the 'spank first and ask questions later' kind of guy, but this was more than just a simple eye roll or rude remark. I have never had to help my girl overcome the guilt of having her man alive and well while her friend had to lay her husband in the ground." He peeked at the clock as he continued. "I have to be at my appointment with my physical therapist in an hour and a half, so I cannot help you with the guilt until this afternoon."

Autumn's pout only lasted for a second before she found her position significantly changed. The minimal amount of effort it took on his part to get her ass in the air and poised for his hand spoke volumes to the both of them in regards to how much she needed this. Even with her need for discipline, the protests still fell from her lips. "You just said you couldn't help with the guilt until after your doctor appointment."

"I can't help you with the guilt until this afternoon," Leland repeated as he rubbed her panty-covered butt. When Autumn tried to get up, he pushed her back down with a firm hand on her shoulder blades and continued. "You made it clear I have been slacking when it comes to my Domly duties, and for that, I am also sorry."

"We have had a lot going on these past couple of months. I accept your apology." She attempted to rise again. When she felt his fingers slide into her panties, she pled over her shoulder, "Sir?"

Without stopping the slow descent of her underwear, he answered the question written all over her face. "I said I couldn't help you with your guilt until this afternoon, and I will, as soon as I get home from the doctor. However, I am remedying my lapse in correcting my sub right now."

"But I didn't—"

Leland looked from her ass to her face. His brown eyes were alive with sparks, just daring her to argue. "I suggest you think before you talk, princess. I may have botched my duties as your Dom these past few weeks, but that ends this morning. Now, we deal with the blatant disrespect of the past few minutes, which you so helpfully brought to my attention. This afternoon, I'll help you with your misplaced guilt." Autumn groaned even as the relief of knowing he still cared relaxed her body. Leland didn't speak again until her panties had completed their descent and were just below her knees. "Why are you over my lap, pet?"

The no-nonsense baritone of his voice sent a shiver down through her body. "Because I pushed, taunted, and bratted you in order to get a reaction out of you, and now you are going to make sure I don't do it again."

"I want specifics." With a feather soft touch, he ran his finger-tips over her bottom, causing goose bumps to form.

"I rolled my eyes at you twice, and I called you Dom Dom, Sir."

"Which means what, sub?"

"Dumb Dom, Sir."

"Did you think I would not know what that meant?"

"I don't know, Sir."

"Well, I assure you, pet, I am no Dom Dom." As soon as he spoke, his hand left her bottom, and Autumn felt his body shift toward his side of the bed.

Autumn gulped, knowing that he was reaching for the drawer of the nightstand and what implements it held. The cool wood settled on her bottom, and the prayer fell from her lips. "Please, not the brush."

"Your plea tells me I have made the correct implement choice." The brush rose, and Autumn had just enough time to anticipate the attack before it returned to her flexed posterior. "If you clench, you will bruise easier. Relax your ass and take the punishment like you know how!"

"Are you kidding? How am I supposed to relax with you smacking my ass with that evil piece of wood?"

"You are right, princess," Leland agreed as he brought the brush down hard on her butt. "I have obviously been slacking in my 'Domly' ways because you know better than to talk to me that way." The brush connected three more times, drawing a cry from her throat before he spoke again. "But here you are, bare assed across my lap, and you are still lipping off. I have a remedy for that." As soon as he finished talking, the brush started its relentless assault, jumping from one cheek to the next.

When Autumn started kicking, Leland merely paused in his assault on her butt, put his leg over hers, and continued with the task at hand like he didn't have a fully grown adult woman struggling with all her might across his lap. A few seconds later, without thought or how foolish and ill-advised the act was, she reached her hands back to protect herself. He paused again, gathered her wrists in his hand and held them in a secure grip at the small of her back before he proceeded with the task at hand. The realization that she was well and truly trapped gave her pause for a second before her mouth got the best of her.

"Fuck!" As soon as the word toppled out of her mouth, she scrambled to take it back. "I'm sorry, I didn't mean that! I'm sorry! I'm so—"

She didn't get to finish her plea for forgiveness before her breath was stolen by the first unrelenting smack of the innocent looking instrument to her delicate sit spot. He applied nine more strikes to the vulnerable crease before he switched to the other side and gave it the same treatment then returned to her butt as if he had never deviated.

It was a struggle to drag air into her lungs once the tears started. They ran down her face as the hiccupping sobs that accompanied them shook her whole body. Leland placed a few more swats before he dropped the brush and gathered her in his arms, smoothly rocking her from side to side.

"Easy, girl. Just let me hold you. Deep breaths, princess. There you go. Do it again."

As the tears slowed, Autumn felt the need to apologize return. "I don't hate you. I promise I don't. I just—"

"I know. You just were mad at me for slacking off, and your mouth got away from you. Your poor sit spots paid profoundly for your lip, didn't they?" When he pushed her from his chest in an attempt to catch her eyes, she instinctively looked to the side. "Eyes."

The growled command and her reddened bottom were enough to get her eyes to snap to his. "I don't think I will sit comfortably for a while."

"You won't, but it will be a good reminder for you when you go see Liv."

Panic settled in Autumn's gut as she felt the blood drain from her face and her breathing speed up. "I can't... I... She... I can't."

"There are two reasons you will do as I tell you." He held up two fingers and ticked them off as he talked. "First, I am in charge, and you don't want to disobey me so soon after a meeting with the brush. Second, you two need each other."

Autumn's head fell to his chest, and she forced herself to copy his breathing pattern. The slow, steady movement helped ease the panic. "I have been a horrible friend."

Leland squeezed her within the circle of his arms. "No, you

have been healing just like the rest of us. You need your friend, and I know she needs the uncensored Autumn."

"Uncensored?"

"You have been tiptoeing around her since shortly after the funeral. That ends today, princess."

Chapter 17

L eland leaned against the side of his truck and held Autumn against his chest with his chin resting on her head. "I have to go. I will be gone a couple of hours. When I pull out of this driveway, I want to see your sore, cute little butt walking to Liv's house. I will pick you up when I come home."

Autumn looked up at the man she loved, even if he was a literal pain in her ass at times. "If I am capable of walking to her house, I am sure I can find my way back. She only lives across the street, Lee. I can manage."

She jumped when he gave her ass a hard pinch. "I will pick you up. Not because I wanted a smart aleck remark, but because I don't want you using me as an excuse to leave."

"Yes, Sir," she replied, watching his brow return to its natural position.

He assaulted her lips with his own unrelenting mouth then stepped away and climbed into his truck. "Get moving, princess."

Autumn kicked a pebble across the street as she stepped away from the truck. She was headed up Liv's driveway before Leland stopped at the bottom of the drive and spoke in a soothing voice through the open window. "You are dragging your feet as if you are walking to your execution rather than your friend's house. Autumn, you are going to comfort and be comforted by a woman who loves you with all her heart. Relax, baby."

Autumn stared back at him. "What if she can't forgive me?"

"Then you give her no choice. I love you."

Autumn watched as the truck turned down a side road and drove away, only looking away when a cloud of gravel dust was all she could see. She continued her journey up the long driveway, and before it seemed possible, she was in front of Liv's door.

She just stood there, staring at the door, trying to get the words tumbling around in her head to line up and make sense. She gave up her attempt to organize her scrambled brain and raised her hand to knock but froze just as her knuckles were about to make contact with the door.

Have things changed this much? Liv is one of my best friends, and I am going to knock on the door? I never knock.

Her arm dropped to her side as her knees buckled. The pain of the solid, unrelenting concrete tearing open the skin on her knees crumbled the feeble wall that held her emotions in check. Her head collided with the bottom of the door as she folded her chest over her knees and allowed the tears to flow, her forehead resting on the cement in front of her.

The impact of her head against the door must have announced her presence as the door was abruptly swung open, and Autumn watched as Liv collapsed to the floor in front of her.

Liv took her hand and pulled her into the house and her arms. They sat in the open doorway wrapped in each other's arms and cried. They cried for the lost life, the lost love and the loss of the future Liv would never get to have with Kevin.

AUTUMN SHIFTED AGAIN, trying to get comfortable, but every

move she made reminded her of Lee's displeasure. It wasn't a horrible pain, but the ache was persistent, and after sitting on the kitchen floor for over an hour, she needed to move.

"Why haven't I seen you since the funeral?" Guilt rolled through Autumn's stomach. Liv must have seen the emotion on her face because before she could open her mouth and let the lie so effortlessly fall from her lips, Liv cautioned, "Don't lie to me."

"I couldn't face you. I couldn't let you see my emotions." When Liv sat there, waiting for her to continue, she took a deep breath and went on, "I felt guilty."

"Why would you feel guilty?"

"Leland survived because Kevin chose Lee over himself." The sharp pain had registered on her cheek before Autumn realized Liv had moved. "I..." She couldn't tell who was more shocked by the assault—her, as she put her hand over the offended side of her face or Liv, who had covered her mouth in shock.

"I'm sorry! Oh, my God, Autumn, I am so sorry!"

"It's okay."

"No! No, it's not! I hit you!"

Autumn leaned forward to pry Liv's hands from in front of her face and forcibly hold them in her own. "Why did you hit me?"

"I don't know."

"Why did you hit me, Liv?" Autumn asked again. Her voice held a little more force.

"I don't know. It… it just happened, and I am *so* sorry."

"Stop apologizing and tell me why did you hit me, Olivia!"

The use of her full name caused something to snap into place, and the truth fell from her mouth as she pounded her fists against Autumn's thighs to emphasize her anger. "Because that was a *stupid* reason to avoid me for over a month! I just lost my husband! My *rock*! I *needed* you, Autumn, and you *selfishly* avoided me because… because you felt *guilty*? What did you have to feel *guilty* about?" Liv's torso crumpled, her head landing in the other woman's lap.

Autumn ran her fingers through Liv's tangled, neglected hair. "I'm sorry. You're right. You needed me, and I intentionally avoided you. I was selfish and a horrible friend, and for that, I am sorry. I am so sorry, but I am here now."

The sound of muffled sniffles filled the room for a few minutes before Liv stood, pulled her friend to her feet and hauled her into the master bedroom. "We need to clean the dirt and pebbles from your scraped knees before they scab anymore." Liv disappeared into the bathroom and took some of Autumn's guilt with her.

She stared at herself in the mirror on the back of Liv's closet door. Her eyes were puffy from all the crying, and she had a Liv sized handprint on her left cheek, but with the guilt beginning to dissipate, she could see some of the light coming back into her eyes.

"Sit down, so I can take care of your scraped knees," Liv commanded as she strolled from the bathroom with an enormous first-aid kit clutched in her hands.

One glance at the perfectly made up bed had a blush spreading across Autumn's face and a small smile turning up the corner of her lips. "I can't. Lee took the brush to me before I came over. It still hurts to sit."

"We just sat on the hard kitchen floor for at least an hour."

"I know, but that was an emotional hour. I didn't notice how much my sit spots hurt until I started to move again."

"Oh, the sit spots are the worse! I hate when Kevin spanks..." Liv abruptly stopped speaking, and her eyes went from joyful to tear filled in a matter of seconds.

"I'm sorry. I shouldn't have brought it up. I'm sorry." Autumn gathered her friend in her arms and let her cry.

After a few minutes, Liv pushed away from Autumn's chest, sniffled and wiped her nose on the sleeve of the button-down flannel shirt that was noticeably three sizes too big. *Kevin's*. "Don't be sorry. We have both said that way too many times today. I forget he isn't coming back sometimes, but when I suddenly remember, it hits me like a ton of bricks." The strong woman stepped out of Autumn's arms and gave herself a visible shake before she headed back to the bathroom, tossing another command over her shoulder. "Bend over the bed. I will put some cream on your butt, and *then* I will clean the dirt out of your scrapes."

Autumn snorted as she did as she was told. She knew better than to think she could argue with Liv while she was in nurse mode.

A laugh bounced off the walls. "I don't think the lotion will do any good if I put it on the back of your shorts. They need to come down."

"Sorry," Autumn said as she stood and wiggled her shorts just low enough that Liv would be able to get lotion on the tender crease below her cheeks. She jumped a bit when Liv started to rub the cream in, but she settled as soon as it started to soothe.

The laughter that echoed through the room a few minutes later was much deeper than Liv's, and both women jumped just as a hand was placed on Autumn's back to keep her in position. "What do we have here? I go to the doctor to get cleared to go back work, and this is what I walk in on?" Leland teased as he ran his fingers up and down Autumn's still bare ass.

Autumn struggled for only a second before she was let up and quickly righted her clothes. "Lee! You scared the crap out of us!" With her shorts where they were supposed to be, Autumn looked at Leland for the first time and saw his eyes immediately darken.

"What happened to your face?" he demanded.

"Umm." Autumn saw her friend take a step back, unintentionally drawing the unhappy man's attention.

"Olivia?"

"I slapped her." Her voice broke, and she took one more step back before she straightened her spine and continued. "She self-ishly avoided me when I needed her. When she told me why, I was so mad that I slapped her before I could talk myself out of it." Leland gathered Liv in his arms and held her. "What am I going to do? I can sense myself starting to spin out of control. I have no one to pull me back in."

"Where is the letter you were given with his flag?"

Liv looked at Lee in confusion. "You mean the letter from the department? It's in the display case behind the flag. I couldn't bring myself to open it and read all the ways you guys were sorry for my loss."

"Liv, honey, that letter was not from the department. All the guys at the station have written a letter to our spouse, just in case the worse ever happened. That is the letter Kevin wrote you." When Olivia ran from the room, Leland turned to Autumn. "She cannot be alone when she reads the letter, but I want you to go home. I'm going to call Jensen to stay with her. I will be home after he gets here. We'll work on appeasing the rest of your guilt when I get there."

"I want to stay. She might need me."

"No," Leland commanded as he grabbed her arm to prevent her from following the sounds of her friend's cries. "It is only going to create more guilt for you. You are going home."

As soon as she opened her mouth to argue, his hand came down on her rear. "Ow!"

"If I had not walked in on Liv putting cream on your ass, I might have actually believed that spank hurt." Autumn's scowl did nothing but earn her another swat as he pushed her out the door. "Go home. I'll be there as soon as Jensen gets here. I expect to find you bent over the arm of the sofa."

Chapter 18

"Don't you dare stand," Leland called as he strolled in the front door. Autumn's belly flipped as she settled back over the arm of the couch. He knew her too well. His hand slid across her ass before he took hold of her yoga pants on either side of her hips and roughly pulled them to her ankles, leaving her barely there panties in place. "Did I not make it clear that you were to be bare to me? And you changed?"

The cool breeze from the air conditioner combined with the recognizable thread of dominance in Leland's voice sent a shiver down her spine. "Yes, Sir, I changed, and you didn't tell me to be naked, Sir. You only said to be over the arm of the sofa when you got home."

"Have you ever been bent over like this and been allowed the privilege of clothing covering your ass?"

"No, Sir," Autumn replied as she felt his finger run up the crack of her butt, the thin fabric of her underwear the only thing keeping him from touching her asshole. "But I didn't want to assume that was what you wanted, Sir. I remember the lesson after the last time I assumed."

"Good girl," Leland praised as he lifted her head and placed a throw pillow beneath it. "I am going to go take a shower. You are to stay here and not move an inch." Autumn watched as he walked away. Stripping as he went, he provided her a quick glimpse of his sculpted glutes.

She felt herself relax into her submission. He was in charge, and she had no decisions to make. She only had to do as she was told, and that was exactly what she needed.

The sounds of the water turning on in the other room drew her attention. The need to join him in the shower grew, but thankfully, her need to submit and please her man was much greater than her need to see his wet, naked body. However, that didn't stop her from torturing herself with a combination of memories and fantasies. Leland wet in the shower with soap bubbles running off his body.

Would he take his cock in hand, working it in his fist? The image of him doing just that sent a shiver down her spine. She almost reached between her legs for relief. While she was able to stop herself from acting on that impulse, she couldn't help but wiggle over the arm of the sofa in an attempt to find just the slightest bit of friction.

The hand that bounced harshly off her ass had her screeching in pain. "Didn't I tell you to stay still, princess?"

She struggled to speak without giving away how turned on she was. "Yes, Sir, you did."

"Then why are you so obviously trying to rub your thighs together to relieve some of the built-up tension in your clit?"

Is that a teasing tone I hear? "I'm sorry, but I was picturing you touching yourself in the shower, and it was all I could do to stop myself from riding my fingers to oblivion." She heard the tiniest catch in his breath as she quickly added, "Sir."

"You are mighty brave for a woman who is currently lying half naked over the arm of my couch, aren't you, sub?" He slowly drew his hand across her nates to emphasize his point.

"Possibly, Sir, but right now it's a risk I'm willing to take if it means I'm getting the attention I desire from the man I love."

His hand rained down on her bottom repeatedly with wild, solid spanks before he demanded, "Say it again!"

She panted with the effort it took her to keep still during the brief assault on her bottom. "Sir?"

He yanked her panties down to join her pants and swiftly pulled them both off her. Roughly, he kicked her feet apart with his foot and gave her pussy a solid spank. A moan fell from her mouth. "Not that. Say it again!"

That single swat forced more need to pour from her depths and muddle her brain. The combined effects almost kept her from asking her question. "Sir, I don't know what you want me to repeat."

"Say you love me again."

She hadn't realized she had said she loved him. "Shit!" She had taken too long to speak, and he was applying smack after smack to her lower lips, her moisture causing the second set of slaps to hurt all the more. After six well-placed swats, she was finally able to find her voice. "I love you!"

His hand rested on her wet, swollen core. "Again."

She turned her head to look at him. He was only wearing a pair of athletic shorts, which were straining to hold his erection at bay. She pulled her eyes from the tent in his shorts and found his. If the animated look in his eyes was anything to go by, he was obviously struggling to hold himself at bay. "I love you, Leland."

"Again." He started a slow agonizing swirl around her swollen clit.

"I love you with every fiber of my being, Leland Boisy."

His hand disappeared a second before he shoved his shorts down and stepped behind her. He crudely buried his cock inside her core. His need was palpable as he buried himself to the hilt and nearly pulled all the way out then plunged in again. "It is about *damn* time I heard those words from your mouth again."

"Again?" Autumn grunted at he pounded into her relentlessly, forcing the couch forward with every thrust of his hips.

Her question was ignored as he gathered her hair in his fist. He pulled her tresses back, forcing her to arch her spine to alleviate the pain in her scalp. Pressing his chest into her back without letting up on his hold, he bit her ear before he whispered harshly into it, "Proclaim your love for me again. I want to hear you say it while I have my dick buried inside you." He slapped the outside of her thigh. The pain quickly morphed into pleasure, forcing her to clamp down on the rapidly moving appendage. "Don't you *dare* come without permission, princess, and you won't receive it until I hear the words."

"I love you, Sir," she cried out breathlessly as the sofa finally hit the wall, ending their slow trek across the living room.

"No," Leland growled, slapping her other thigh with so much force there was no doubt there would be a handprint. It took everything she had to keep herself from tumbling into oblivion. "I want to hear my name fall from those beautiful lips of yours."

"I love you, Leland! I love you, I love you, I love you! Now, for God's sake, may I *please* come?"

One of Leland's hands left her hip, and he forced it between her body and the couch, tapping lightly on her hidden button. "Now, baby!" he commanded as he harshly flicked her clit. As her body convulsed, she felt him bury himself deep within her. He stilled, and a grunt fell from his mouth.

Chapter 19

Autumn snuggled deeper into Leland's chest. They were sitting on the sofa, his back against the armrest and his legs stretched the length of the couch. He held Autumn curled against his chest, neither of them wearing a stitch of clothing. He ran the tip of his index finger over the outside of her hip. "You have a couple of gorgeous handprints on your legs, princess."

She let the sass drip from her words but didn't bother to lift her head off his chest. "Hmm, I wonder how those got there?"

"When you don't follow directions, and I cannot reach your disobedient ass because I am hammering into your hot pussy I, as your Dom, have no choice but to deliver swift justice to another accessible part of your body. If you would have just done as you were told, you would still have pasty white thighs."

She lifted her head from his chest—her mouth open in shock and her eyes slightly narrowed. "I don't have pasty white thighs! Besides, if you weren't so lost in your caveman mode and able to form more than single word sentences, I may have understood what you wanted me to say before you felt the need to smack my delicate flesh."

"Laying it on a bit thick, princess."

She laid her head back down. "This is what I missed the most."

"Laying your head on my hairy chest?"

"No." Autumn lightly smacked his chest. "I missed how much a scene brings us together."

"That was nothing like the scene I had planned."

"So? It was the scene we both needed."

Leland tipped her chin up so he could see her eyes. "Did it help with your guilt?"

"No."

The disappointment registered on his face. "I am so sorry, baby. We will figure this out together. We will find a way to deal with your emotions."

"Let me finish," Autumn mildly chided. "I didn't realize it until I got home from Liv's, but she was the person I needed to forgive me the most, and I got that forgiveness right before she slapped me across the face for being selfish." Leland's growl made Autumn snicker. "What I needed from you was to know you still wanted to be my Dom because I need to submit. Yes, we have had sex since the fire, but you didn't take control at all. You let me have all the power. I decided the position. I set the pace. I called a halt to it when I wanted. It was the worst sex we have ever had, solely because I was unable to get out of my head and just do as you ordered. I needed you to take back your power in order for me to know you forgave me. After the session this morning and a few minutes ago, mission accomplished."

Confusion was evident in both Leland's voice and on his face. "Why would you need my forgiveness?"

Tears gathered in Autumn's eyes, and her voice broke before she was able to answer him. "If you had not needed to scold me for helping the cops with the father, you would have been nowhere near the house when the wall fell. He would have never needed to make the decision between you or himself. He could have saved himself. Liv would have her husband. You would be free to live your life without the knowledge that your best friend gave up his life and future for you." With swift, determined movements, Lee changed positions and had her across his lap before she'd even realized he had sat up. "Lee, what?" Her sentence was cut short when his hand met her ass.

"Do you think I would blame you for the choice of another adult?"

"It was my fault." An extra hard spank landed on the back of her thigh. "If I had just followed protocol and stayed away, like the rest of the paramedics, you both would be okay."

Leland had landed another volley of swats on her rapidly coloring skin before his voice mingled with the steady sound of the flesh meeting flesh. "You are right." Autumn's heart sank, and she went limp over his lap. "Let me finish. You are right. You should have followed protocol. Truthfully, I am very surprised you didn't get more than a week's suspension for ignoring scene safety, but you are also wrong." Leland stopped spanking and rested his hand on her heated flesh. "Listen carefully, Autumn Rose. I have not, do not and never will blame you for the tragic accident that took Kevin's life. We will never know what was running through his head when he decided to give up his life for me, but I do know if he were here now, he would have taken you over his knee weeks ago, right after he knocked some sense into me via a well-placed boot for failing to see what you needed sooner."

Autumn snorted with laughter as Leland helped her to sit on his lap and snuggle into his chest again. "Could you imagine what he would have done once he found out Liv slapped me? If you keep growling like that, I am going to have to call animal control."

"Sorry, princess, but every time I think about the handprint on your face, I become sick to my stomach." He ran his hand over the cheek that had been assaulted. "I know what he would have done. The poor girl would have sat gingerly for at least a week. Same as you if I ever hear you blaming yourself for Kevin's death again."

"Don't worry, Sir," Autumn assured, running her fingers through his chest hair. "As I said, my guilt is gone, but if it comes back, I will tell you rather than let it stew. Promise."

"Good girl."

Epilogue

I *could not be any more of a cliché if I tried.*

There he was, the villain, standing in shadows of the alley behind an apartment building. At least in the movies, the bad guy got to see the woman he was stalking. He had only seen his target once since he'd arrived three hours ago, and he was getting sick of standing there.

Turning into the building, the man dug a pack of smokes from his pocket and lit one with a deep inhale. He hated smoking, but the need was too great.

That was why he was sitting in the dark alley at three in the morning. His need. He needed to see her. The news reporter who first told the world of his talents. He needed her to do it again and again and again. She needed to share his work with the world. Show them the power he held within. Force the people to take notice. He could not be forgotten again.

He pressed himself against the wall a bit more when a car pulled to a stop at the end of the alleyway. With the glow of the streetlight illuminating the driver's face, he could just make out who it was.

"Seems my girl is popular among the men," he mumbled

before turning from the new arrival to the car that had been parked in his girl's parking spot for the past few nights. It wasn't hers. According to the snooping he had done, she didn't own a car.

It had taken hours of surveillance, but he had finally gotten a glimpse of the owner the night before last. He had noticed two things about the man, he was older than she was and he was married. The silver in his hair and on his finger had reflected the light of the well-lit parking lot.

He had thought him to be her father, at first, but he had never seen a grown woman greet her father by taking a running leap into his arms. He had thought his girl was better than that.

If there wasn't such a risk of the search being traced back to him, he would run the plates, get the home address, and warn the poor, unsuspecting woman, but he had to be careful. Helping a scorned woman was an unnecessary risk.

The car at the end of the alley started up, and he turned to watch it pull away. He didn't like the man, Zander. Maybe he should make him his next target. It would surely keep the reporter connected to the story. After all, she had loved him. Why, was beyond him, but he saw it in her eyes every time she looked at the cocky man, and it infuriated him.

The pieces of his plan came together like a puzzle in his head. The smile that spread across his face was sinister.

The sneer stayed in place as he strode away from the building, dropping the butt as he went. He had a plan to work out and an arsonist to get rid of.

After all, all of her attention needed to be on him.

THE END

Rachel Blake

I have been writing since high school, but truthfully never thought it would go any further than a few short stories hidden deep within my laptop. It wasn't until my family moved away from everything we knew that I started writing stories worth sharing. Now, my husband, three kids, our plethora of animals, and I live in the Midwest. When I'm not running around like your stereotypical soccer mom (sans the minivan) I am writing the type of stories I have always secretly treasured: love stories with a sexy alpha and a strong submissive counterpart.

Follow her here:
https://www.facebook.com/AuthorRachelBlake

Don't miss these exciting titles by Rachel Blake and Blushing Books!

Hill City Heroes
Fire Princess - Book One

CPSIA information can be obtained
at www.ICGtesting.com
Printed in the USA
LVHW091628010320
648615LV00002B/389